West of Tombstone

West of Tombstone, Arizona, the land turns harsh and savage. Here are gila monsters, sidewinders and peccaries, and, above all, the sun glares like white fire over the waterless waste. But none of these is as dangerous as the men who live upon the desert, who'll cut your throat for a dollar or for your boots and smile as they are doing it.

A man does not cross these deserts alone, but for a man like Cameron Black there is no other chance for survival. When you have managed to cheat the hangman's rope at Yuma prison and your pursuers believe you hold the key to fifty thousand dollars in gold, you ride on until you can ride no more. . . .

By the same author

The Devil's Canyon
The Drifter's Revenge

West of Tombstone

Owen G. Irons

A Black Horse Western

ROBERT HALE · LONDON

© Owen G. Irons 2006
First published in Great Britain 2006

ISBN-10: 0-7090-7949-4
ISBN-13: 978-0-7090-7949-1

Robert Hale Limited
Clerkenwell House
Clerkenwell Green
London EC1R 0HT

Typeset by
Derek Doyle & Associates, Shaw Heath
Printed and bound in Great Britain by
Antony Rowe Limited, Wiltshire

ONE

West of Tombstone the land turns harsh and bitter, sere and savage. The men who live in that wasteland are no different. Maybe it's the country that makes them so hard. They'll cut your throat for a dollar, or for your boots, and smile as they are doing it. There are coyotes, Gila monsters and sidewinders in the desert, dangerous creatures to be sure, but not so dangerous as the men. They merely live as they were intended to live. As for the men, well, that is the way they choose to live.

You do not cross those deserts alone and expect to survive. They are crossed because a man has no other choice, no other chance for survival. When you have managed to cheat the hangman's rope then even that wild and dangerous freedom is miles ahead of the swift descent to hell you have been expecting. . . .

*

Cameron Black rode on.

The sun was sinking in the west and he tugged his hat lower. Beneath him the pinto horse had begun to drag its feet wearily. It wasn't Cameron Black's horse. He had stolen it. As he had stolen the Henry repeating rifle riding in its scabbard under his right knee. Horse stealing was still a hanging offense in Arizona Territory.

But it didn't matter – they can only hang you once.

The sky was flaming scarlet and brilliant orange as it began its slow slide to some resting place beyond the saw-toothed mountains ahead of Cameron. Doves winged their way homeward, cutting quick shadows against the purple sky. A coyote looked up in surprise and slunk away, its prey – a jack-rabbit – in its jaws. At least the coyote would eat that evening. At least the doves would find water. Cameron would have neither.

The paint pony stumbled from exhaustion and Cameron Black halted the weary animal to swing down to the desert sand. There was a breeze, hot and gusting, rising with the sunset. He removed his hat and wiped off his forehead with his shirt cuff. His hair was dry before he put his hat back on. His shirt and jeans were caked white with sweat. The noon temperature had probably been near 110°. It wasn't much cooler now, even with the sun fading to a faintly glowing golden memory. He walked on; there was nothing else to do.

Water was all that he needed. Enough water to keep the paint horse moving. They had to get off the desert floor and into the foothills which bulked against the Arizona sky. Water was life. Without it he and the horse both would end up a pile of bleached bones, torn apart by the scavengers, like the remains he had occasionally passed of oxen some fool wayfarer had tried to drive across this wasteland.

Night had fallen and the darkness was nearly complete. A hazy purple glow illuminated the far mountain range dimly and the stars were bright enough for Cameron to see a few individual stark forms against the sky, like the tall saguaro cactus appearing in the darkness like startled bandits with their hands raised. The volcanic rocks with their jagged edges, the catclaw and the nopal cactus he could not see, and stumbling once into a patch of them he had decided that he had no choice but to stop for the night.

He unfastened the twin cinches on the Texas-rigged saddle and wearily dropped it to the sand. The saddle blanket he placed over it. This was his pillow for the night. Sagging to the earth he looked to the long lonely skies and then hung his head wearily. Later a thin crescent moon would rise above the saw-toothed range, bringing a thin silver sheen to the sandy waste, but it did not matter. He could travel no farther tonight.

There were *tinajas* – stony catch basins – out there, somewhere on the desert, but he did not know the land that well. Stony Harte had known where they were, all the tiny seeps and springs that could keep a man and his horse alive in the wasteland, but Stony was not here. Stony was nowhere at all, or perhaps he wandered somewhere between this world and the netherlands, seeking his gold.

Stony was the reason Cameron Black wandered the broad, lifeless desert, the reason Hell had descended upon him.

A scant twelve days earlier, Cameron's life had seemed bright and full of promise, well, as full of promise as it ever had seemed since he had begun his wandering ways. Since then he had been shot at, arrested, sentenced to be hanged, escaped from prison and become lost on the desert. All thanks to Stony. A man should choose his friends more carefully.

Cameron stretched out on the sand which was still hot and would be crowded with scorpions and night-hunting predators once his presence was sensed. He painfully raised his head onto his saddle and stared gloomily at the suddenly brilliant mass of stars overhead. His eyes closed slowly, inexorably as the tremendous heat of the day faded to the numbing cold of the desert night and he recalled it all before he finally, fitfully, fell to sleep.

'Stony Harte,' the grinning young man on the leggy gray pony had said, thrusting out his hand.

Cameron had taken it and nodded to the bright-eyed, curly-haired cowboy. They sat their ponies side by side, letting them drink from the thin silver creek. Overhead, willow trees offered their tenuous shade to the travelers. Gnats rose in clouds around them and had to be fanned away. Above the ribbon of bright water, dragonflies, blue and orange, sped this way and that on silken wings. Cicadas sang enthusiastically in the brush.

'I'm Cameron Black.'

'Nice to meet you, Cam,' Harte said. He tilted his battered hat back and surveyed the long white land surrounding them. 'Do you know how far it is to Tombstone?'

'Maybe thirty miles,' Cameron answered.

'Well, that's not too bad if Dolly here doesn't get cantankerous on me.' He patted the neck of the big gray mare he rode. The horse had a white mane and tail and a menacing expression in her eye.

'Is she hard to manage?' Cameron asked.

'Hard to manage?' Harte laughed. 'I should say so, but she'll run all day and all night so long as I keep reminding her who's boss. She's a tough old gal.'

'You have business in Tombstone?' Cameron asked, and Harte laughed again.

'No, sir, I sure don't. I mean to stay as far away from that town as possible. I was just wondering.'

Black nodded. Had Harte crossed someone there? Was it woman trouble? He didn't know, but in those times it was not considered polite to ask a man what lay behind him. The Civil War and the Kansas trouble were too near in memory. Men on every branch of the spectrum wandered here and there, most of them using assumed names or none at all.

'I have some pemmican,' Harte said, 'and a little coffee. Could I invite you to dinner?'

'You could,' Cameron said. 'I'm riding to Tombstone with a sackful of beans, a little bacon, a couple ounces of coffee and little more.'

'You have an opportunity up there?' Harte asked, as the two men led their ponies back into the lacy shade of a clump of towering mesquite where the insects were swarming.

'No,' Cameron Black admitted. 'It's just a place to be. Another place to be.'

Stony Harte questioned him no further. He went to the saddle-bags his pony carried and removed the pemmican he had. Pounded veni-son it was, with some sort of berry Cameron

10

didn't recognize by taste ground into it – sour oak berries, likely, and a hint of sage. They sat on Harte's blanket watching the silver glitter of the tiny stream, eating silently as a coffee pot boiled over dry willow twigs. They could hear quail chuckling to each other in the thick brush. A lone vulture circled overhead, awaiting the death of some unseen desert creature. If the animal it was watching died, dozens, perhaps hundreds of the birds would arrive in a long dark wave from their hiding place.

'Filthy beasts,' Harte said, watching the huge soaring bird. 'I hate them.'

He was propped up on one elbow, hat tilted back, sipping his roughly brewed coffee from a tin cup.

Cameron was struck by how much the stranger resembled him. Both had slightly curly dark hair, although Stony Harte's was streaked with thin strands of silver. Similar in height, they both had gray eyes. They could have been brothers. Stony, however, was more outgoing, more prone to laughter. Cameron Black was of a serious nature. He had the right to be, considering his background.

'So?' Stony asked, stretching his arms, yawning. 'Ride west together or not? If you don't find me bad company, it might be better for both of us. They tell me the Jicarilla Apaches are stirring up some dust out there.'

'I've nothing against it,' Cameron said. There was some hesitance in his tone, but Stony seemed not to notice it. Cameron liked the man well enough, but in those days it was still considered reckless to ride the wasteland with strangers. No matter – what did he have to lose, after all? And if the Indians did decide to take a crack at them, two men with guns were definitely better than finding oneself alone on the desert.

'Good,' Stony said, flashing his bright smile, thrusting out his hand again. 'That's settled, then.' They unsaddled their ponies and let them pick at the scant grass and the mesquite beans. It was poor forage, but both horses were in good condition and they could survive on what they could scavenge for another day or so. Stony had said that he knew this section of the desert intimately, every seep and *tinaja* where good water could be found. That was all they would truly need. Without water every man, beast and plant was doomed to perish in this country.

Stony's manner was so confident that one could not doubt him. He told stories of hidden meadows and lost springs known only to the Indians, of secret caverns in the red mesas where a man could sit out the torrid heat of the desert day, of friends he had made among the nomadic tribes, and hinted at small Mexican pueblos where he had many *amigos* and lovers with huge dark eyes.

It was easy to believe Stony Harte, impossible not to like this roaming gregarious cowboy. Before the moon had risen, Cameron slept rolled up tightly in his blanket against the chill of the desert night. Something awakened him. His horse pawing at the sandy earth, the far-distant howl of a lonely coyote. . . . Opening one eye he watched by the faint starlight as Stony Harte slipped from his bed and went to his horse, removing the saddle-bags from its back. When he returned stealthily to his bed, he doubled the bags and, using them as a pillow, lay down again. As he did, the saddle-bags gave out an audible metallic clink and then settled. Cameron Black closed his eyes and considered this, but determining that it was none of his business, he rolled over and fell back to sleep with the cold stars shimmering overhead across the long, white desert floor.

The nudge of a boot toe against his ribs brought Cameron awake. He pawed at his eyes, crusty from the dust off the salt flat and saw a silhouette standing over him, outlined against crystal stars and a blue-black sky. He tensed and reached for his revolver before remembering that he now had a new traveling companion.

'Stony?' he muttered, relaxing.

'Who else? Better roll out and saddle your pony.'

'Good God! What time is it?' Cameron grumbled. There was not a trace of dawn light in the sky; no breeze blew across the long desert. The temperature had plummeted overnight as it does on the desert with no clouds to hold the terrible heat of the day.

'Just told you,' Stony answered, with a grin Cameron could not see. 'My friend, it'll be ninety degrees by mid-morning and we have miles to go. Let's hit the trail while we can.'

Sitting up, Cameron rubbed his head and stared unblinkingly at the darkness. Then, shrugging, he rose and with his blanket still over his shoulders went to slip the bit to his reluctant paint pony and saddle it. The smell of coffee was rich and inviting on the morning air as he walked back to the camp. Harte had started a small fire with mesquite twigs and was boiling something less than two cups of coffee. Cameron squatted down beside him, yawing. Harte passed him a tin cup of coffee across the embers.

'I shouldn't have started the fire,' Stony said, sipping at his own coffee. 'Out here flame can be seen a long way. The coffee can be smelled almost as far.'

'There's no one around to smell it,' Cameron said.

'No?' Stony's eye narrowed. 'My friend, an Apache could be lying behind a sandhill not twenty feet from us right now and you wouldn't see him, nor would you have heard him approach in his moccasins. Some fools will sit around smoking tobacco as well – do you know how far away that can be smelled! Ask somebody who doesn't smoke. The 'Paches know when something isn't right. This is their country after all.'

'You seem to know the Apaches well,' Cameron commented. He had caught himself unconsciously searching the perimeter of the camp for shadows that should not be there.

'Not really. As well as most white men do, I guess,' Stony replied, 'and that's not well at all when you come to think of it. No,' he said more definitely, 'I don't know 'em. But I know how they hunt, how they track and how they fight. I know just enough to have kept me alive this long out here.'

Stony rose silently. Cameron saw him look toward the east and then he began kicking sand over the faintly glowing embers, putting the fire out. 'I can see a ribbon of gray above the horizon. It's time we were traveling.'

They rode for a few miles across hard-baked playa with an infinity of cracks separating the brittle salt flats into plate-sized segments as the sun slowly rose and stretched long crooked shadows of man and horse out before them. Nothing grew here, not even scrub chaparral or impervious cactus. Within an hour the sun had grown to an angry crimson hue and the white salt flats absorbed the color and turned it back on them like seeming red mirrors. To Cameron it seemed that they were veering toward the west, away from Tombstone and he asked Stony about it.

'We need to reach Maricopa Creek,' Stony said, lifting his chin toward the north-west. 'It elbows back toward Tombstone. We can't ride far on the playa. The horses would die under us and we'd be next.'

Cameron nodded, thanking his stars that he had run into a man who knew this desert and its secrets. He glanced at Stony Harte as the glare of the sun blurred his vision. Harte wore his gun on his left hip for a cross-handed draw. His hat was broad, doeskin-colored. A fancy band of silver decorated with bits of red and green turquoise, obviously of Navajo Indian craftsmanship, circled the low crown.

His gray horse stepped lightly and, despite Stony's complaint that the gray mare with its white mane and tail was obstinate, Dolly seemed to obey even the slightest pressure of the reins intelligently, without protest. The two were as one and Cameron knew they had ridden many a trail together.

The sun was a burning brand against Cameron's back. By early morning, true to Stony's prediction, the temperature had soared, approaching three figures. The flats, now color-less, stretched out to the border of infinity. Cam's own paint pony seemed to be faltering in the heat.

'Water?' Cameron Black asked, as he and Stony rode side by side in companionable misery.

'We'll hit easier going soon,' Stony answered. He pointed ahead with a gloved hand to where the broken flats began to be encroached upon by wind-scoured sand dunes. It didn't seem to Cameron to be easier going, but anything beat these damned salt flats.

Stony told him, 'Another few miles and we'll find the Maricopa. It's a dry creek this time of year, but there are brackish pools here and there – enough for our purpose.' Which, Cameron decided, was to remain alive beneath the white sun.

They began to see dry, sand-smothered creosote bushes and alkali-coated mesquite. An unpromising vista, but Cam knew it indicated that somewhere near there was at least occasional water. They rode up the flank of a low, overheated dune and Stony Harte lifted a finger without speaking, indicating a line of low dead willows lining a dry river-bed stretching out like a dark thread toward the far horizon.

As they reached flat land again Stony became more talkative.

'Where you from, Cameron?' he asked, thumbing his broad-brimmed hat back off his forehead. 'I hear some Georgia in your voice.'

Cam grinned through chapped lips. 'You have a good ear. Waycross, Georgia, originally.'

'I thought so,' Stony said with a nod. 'Myself I'm from Macon. Funny – two Georgia boys meeting away out here in this damnable country. Far away from the magnolia trees and the oaks hung with those lush skirts of Spanish moss.' His eyes were briefly reminiscent, lost in the memory of the Old South.

'It is. But it's my luck I met you, Stony.'

'Maybe,' Stony Harte said with a suggestion of something Cameron couldn't grasp. The thought slid away, drifting on the dry desert breeze. 'Funny,' he went on, as they neared the dry creek, 'I feel like we've met before.'

Cameron laughed. 'I was thinking at first that we might be related somehow,' he said.

'Who knows? I did notice right off that we bear a resemblance. Hell, maybe we had a great-grandaddy who was a rambling Georgia man!'

They rode now along the bank of the Maricopa. There was not a sign of water. But the polished stones spread from bank to sandy bank indicated that indeed water did flow there at times, probably in torrents as flash floods off the high western hills funneled through its bed. Other signs of water appeared, like fragments of a jigsaw puzzle. A dragonfly lazed past and desert quail emerged from the willow brush, glanced at them and rushed away at their approach, not frightened enough to fly, but cautious enough to seek shelter. Now there were a few green leaves on the twisted branches of the tangled willows and once a cottontail rabbit in their path sat looking at them uncertainly before it too fled.

'Not far now,' Stony Harte said. 'This is called the Contreras spur. There's a pool not far along where there's always enough water for a couple of men and their horses.'

Cameron could only hope that Harte was correct. His tongue clove to his palate and his lower lip had split with the heat and dryness. The paint horse was not moving well at all, not like the nimble and feisty Dolly who continued to obey eagerly the lightest touch of Stony's heel or slightest pressure of his knees.

But then, Cameron thought, Dolly was a desert horse and she trusted her rider. The paint horse that Cameron had purchased in Tucson seemed bewildered by this sere landscape and the long white skies, considering this usage brutal.

At mid-afternoon they came upon the

promised water.

'Let Dolly sample it first,' Stony advised. 'She knows the smell of alkali and the scent of arsenic. If she doesn't back from it, we've got sweet water.'

They swung down from their weary horses and Cameron held his eager paint pony back until Dolly sampled the pond first. She nosed the pond scum away from the brackish surface of the steel gray pool, tasted gingerly and then dropped her muzzle fully to begin drinking deeply. Stony Harte laughed and nodded to Cam to let his own horse drink. After the two men had drunk their fill and replenished their canteens they sagged tiredly to the sandy earth. A bower of tightly woven thorny mesquite and willow brush towered over them, filtering the sunlight. There was a single, ancient sycamore tree, its mottled bough arching low above the pond.

There were red ants streaming in a furious erratic line to the mesquite brush and back to wherever they had their nest, and pond skimmers – those strange long-legged insects which seemed to have the ability to walk on water – a multitude of quail tracks and, as Stony pointed out in the wetter sand near the pool, the hoof prints of a small doe.

'Wish she was here now,' Stony said, removing his hat to wipe his brow. 'I've had all the pemmican I can take. Leave that for the Indians.'

Cameron laughed, agreeing, and asked Stony about making a fire for coffee, but the older man shook his head decisively. 'We're farther into Jicarilla country, Cam. That's a very bad idea.'

Cameron noticed that Stony had chosen to sit on his saddle-bags and not his blanket, but he didn't make a remark. The day remained unwaveringly hot, without a stirring of breeze, but they had the roughly woven shade overhead and the cooling influence of nearby water, and the afternoon was not all that unpleasant. Quail still spoke in the underbrush; perhaps disturbed by this man-presence near their watering place. A ball of gnats hung menacingly in the air but did not move in their direction.

Cameron, the heat and deprivation weighing on him, let his eyes close as he sat on his horse blanket placed over the burning sand. If it were twenty degrees cooler, he thought, he wouldn't mind stretching out for a nap.

'You know, Stony . . .' he began, opening his eyes.

His words were cut off sharply before he could continue, for through the white glitter of the sunlight he saw that Stony Harte had drawn his pistol and had it aimed toward him.

'Stony!' Cameron shouted. Before he could move, Harte pulled the trigger of his .44, the roar echoing thunderously in the small copse. And then Stony Harte laughed out loud as the shot echoed up the canyon and black powdersmoke roiled upward through the tangle of branches into the white desert sky.

TWO

'Learn to watch where you sit,' Stony Harte said with a smile. He had risen to walk toward Cameron Black's blanket. Using his boot toe he nudged the four-foot long sidewinder from the sand. The rattler was dead and, Cameron noticed, it had been killed by the single .44 bullet that had taken its head off neatly. Stony buried the head of the snake with his boot and picked up the sidewinder's rubbery, near-white body which he tossed far away for some other predator to feed on.

Cameron found he was still trembling. It wasn't the snake so much that caused his fear, it was the sudden murderous glint he had glimpsed in the eyes of Stony Harte, as he drew his revolver and fired in one deft movement. *That could have been me*, he thought irrationally as he watched the viper being flung away.

'I never saw him. . . .' Cameron said shakily. 'How did you know?'

'I saw his eyes protruding from the sand. He was watching you. Doubt he would have struck unless you molested him – they usually don't. But,' Stony went on, 'you might have stuck a hand on him while you were rising or shifting position.' He shook his head and smiled again. 'Rattlers don't like that.'

'That shot. . . ?' Cameron Black asked.

'Yeah, we should be moving. If there are Jicarillas around they'll have heard it.' Stony rose, put on his fancy hat and hefted his saddlebags.

It was cooler now and they continued to follow the course of the Maricopa. There was still no running water to be seen in the riverbed, but now and then Cameron could smell moisture in the still hot air. To him it seemed they were continuing to veer north-west, away from Tombstone, but Stony had assured him that the creek bent eventually toward the town. And here they always had the chance of coming across water. Out on the desert flats there was none.

The land began to change again with the passing of the evening hours. Low hills began to appear along their way, studded with agave, their flanks littered with red volcanic stones. Cameron heard an owl hoot somewhere and a rush of motion in the willow brush lining the river as some larger animal took to its heels at their approach.

Purple dusk was beginning to settle and there was a pale, rose-colored narrow pennant of cloud adhering to the sky. Stony asked from out of the near darkness: 'How do you come to find yourself in this country, Cameron?'

'I lost my mother and father at the same time,' Cameron shrugged. 'I was sent to live with an uncle in Arkansas. He didn't like me and I didn't like him. A cousin in Tucson invited me to come West and work on his dry ranch. By the time I got here we were in full drought and there was no water at all for his stock tanks. He had to sell off his cattle to the army and he moved on to New Mexico where a friend had offered him a clerking job in a dry goods store. Me ... I hung around Tucson for a while but there was no work there. I hear they're hiring mule skinners in Tombstone,' he shrugged, 'so that's where I'm headed. If it doesn't work out, I'll travel on again. I got no roots left, no people.

'How about you, Stony?'

Stony Harte's voice was low, controlled, but bitter as he answered out of the near darkness. 'I lost my folks in Georgia too. Mine were killed by Union soldiers. I lost an uncle, two brothers and my aunt lost her mind when the Yankees burned the house down and took over her land.

'I swore I'd never live in the States again. That's how I come to be in Arizona Territory. If it ever becomes a state, I'll move on again – even if it's to Australia.'

The anger was unmistakable, the hatred of the Yankees. Cameron was sorry he had asked the question at all.

Venus, the evening star, had begun to glow dimly above the western horizon. Cameron felt his pony misstep, stumbling on a round creek bottom rock. 'Think maybe we ought to pick a campsite, Stony?' he asked.

'No. We're pushing on a little farther.'

Cameron shrugged and followed along doggedly. It was Stony's country; he must have had some goal in mind. Near the creek now Cameron could tell, by scent, the willows were greener, water more plentiful, and he caught sight of three or four closely growing cottonwood trees not far ahead. Stony beckoned in the darkness and Cameron followed him through the brush and up onto open country without question.

They found themselves on a low bluff where the scent of sagebrush was heavy and clumps of nopal cactus grew here and there. They followed a narrow path no wider than a rabbit run until Stony finally drew Dolly up at the edge of a rise and halted, looking down into the small valley that had appeared. Cameron could make out a tiny cabin, a small grove of live oak trees standing near it. A light burned in the cabin's window.

'You knew this was here,' Cameron said in surprise.

'Sure, Cam! I told you to trust me. Let's go on down.'

'Is it safe? Maybe we should hail the house first.'

'It's all right,' Stony said. His teeth flashed white in the light of the growing starlight. 'They're friends of mine.'

What a blessing it would be to find himself under a roof, Cam was thinking, as they started down the brushy slope, making their way through manzanita and greasewood. They would have some sort of rough meal to offer as well, whoever they were. Possibly even hay, at least some sort of fodder for the weary horses. And water!

It was his great luck that he had managed to fall in with Stony Harte, he reflected. He might have wandered aimlessly on the desert behind them. Worse, he could have encountered the Jicarillas on his own, or simply died from lack of water. Stony was a godsend, this desert nomad who seemed to know every pond and pass, secret trail and mountain divide.

Why then, as they approached the cabin from out of the darkness did Cameron find a cold creeping trepidation pass over him like a warning wind?

Stony halted his horse again when they were fifty yards or so from the small cabin. Putting his cupped hands to his mouth he sounded two owl hoots and was answered from somewhere in the darkness beyond the cabin. Smiling, Stony nodded to Cameron Black and they started on.

Cameron caught a glimpse of a man with a rifle moving toward them slowly from the oak grove, and he wondered briefly why such precautions were necessary. The answer was so obvious that his unease was banished by embarrassment at his own doubts. These people were, after all, occupying a country where the Apaches ranged.

Cameron saw the front door to the cabin open a crack. Then it was flung open, lantern-light flooding the porch as a grinning man without a hair on his head stepped out, pistol in his hand.

'We'd given you up, Stony,' the stranger said cheerfully.

'You know better than to count me out, Slyke,' Stony answered, swinging down from Dolly. He looped the gray horse's reins over the crossbar of the hitch rail and stood, hands on hips, as the man who had emerged from the oaks sauntered up to him.

This one, Cameron saw by the light flooding from the cabin's smoky interior, was tall, red-haired, wearing only his trousers, boots and long john shirt as if he had been roused quickly and dispatched quickly.

'Hello, Willie,' Stony Halle said without offering his hand. The red-head's eyes were black in the darkness and they were fixed on Cameron. His nose, Cam saw, had been badly sliced at one time and had been stitched on carelessly, leaving it crooked and grossly flabby.

'Who's this?' the man named Willie asked.

'Cameron Black. He's a fellow-traveler,' Stony replied, with a small gesture that could have meant anything.

Swinging down from the paint pony's back, Cameron nodded to the two strangers. His uneasiness had returned, but he did not know why. No matter, if they were friends of Stony's, these men had to be accepted. No matter that they appeared tough and cautious. Most men in this territory were understandably cautious around those they did not know.

'Got any coffee?' Stony asked, untying the piggin strings that held his saddle-bags.

'Coffee and white lightning,' the bald man, Slyke, answered.

29

'Then why are you boys making me stand out here in the dark!'

He inclined his head and Cameron followed him into the poorly built shack. Without sawn lumber to be had it had been constructed of whatever was at hand. Adobe clay over poles with a brush and pole roof. Cameron had slept in worse places; he paid no attention to the packed earth floor or darting mosquitoes.

'About time!' said the voice from beneath the Indian blanket in the corner. The blanket was spread over a roughly made low bed with a thin mattress of ticking. When it was thrown back, the woman in the black dress emerged with a quick smile for Stony and a narrow-eyed appraisal of Cameron Black.

'Who is this?' she asked tightly.

By the smoky glow of the kerosene lantern Cameron could not make her out well. Her voice was gravelly and low-pitched. She was quite short and fairly stout. Her hair was a haystack tangle of dark, gray-streaked locks. 'My God!' she murmured, still staring at Cameron. She picked up a brush from a rickety table and began working at her hair with a sort of nervous authority.

'I know, Emily,' Stony said to her. He then tossed the saddle-bags from his shoulder onto her bed and told Slyke, 'I'll have some coffee now. Let me have a straight shooter of that gump you call whiskey first to clear the dust.'

Willie nodded and walked to a corner stove constructed of a few bricks and a sheet of rusty steel. He poked at the smoldering fire and startled a few flames to life. Then he handed Stony a pint jar with an inch or so of pale liquor in it. Cameron was offered nothing.

'What happened to the boys?' Willie asked impatiently. He rubbed at his deformed nose and stared at Cameron as if challenging him to say something about it. Cam's unease had returned, and now it was based more solidly on something beyond suspicions. He had somehow blundered into a band of dangerous men.

Stony drank a neat ounce of poisonous white lightning and shook his head. 'The shotgun rider got Billy even before we had them halted. Some dude inside the stage took it into his head that he was a gunfighter. He leaped out of the Concorde and blasted away at Indian Joe. Missed the first two shots, got him the next.'

'How many did you get, Stony?' the woman asked, her eyes bright with the excitement of the tale.

Stony shrugged and took another drink of the poor whiskey, wiping his lips on his cuff. 'I'm here, ain't I? I got all three of them. I took the shotgun rider with a snap shot; I took my time with the passenger. I always liked Indian Joe. The driver played possum, pretending he'd been hit: I knew he hadn't, so I hit him for real.'

'Only you, Stony,' the stout woman said with frank admiration.

'The trouble is that I think there was another passenger. He bolted out the far door and took to the brush. I didn't have time to search for him – no telling who the shots would bring. I grabbed the payroll and got out of there. I dumped the silver. For its weight it isn't worth that much and I was alone and needing to travel fast. I burned the army scrip. That's worthless. Especially if we decide to head out for Mexico. The gold . . .' He nodded toward the saddle-bags resting on the Indian blanket.

Cameron Black felt himself sway slightly. His worst fears had been realized. He had wandered like a child into the camp of a band of murderous thieves.

'Strange, ain't it?' the woman said. 'The resemblance, I mean,' she said, stepping nearer to Cameron to look at his face. 'Eerie, is what it is – the way he looks like you.' She still held her tortoiseshell brush in her hand. Now she lifted it as if she would tap it against Cam's chest, but she did not. She turned her back and went to Stony and whispered something that made the outlaw grin.

Slyke was seated near the saddle-bags Stony had brought in and now his hand fumbled with the clasps. Stony Harte saw the motion from the corner of his eye and he whirled, his hand on the butt of his pistol.

'Leave that be for now!'

'It's part mine, isn't it?' the bald man said sulkily, but he didn't like the look in Stony's eyes and he rose to turn away.

'Why'd you bring the kid along with you?' Willie demanded, watching Cameron.

'Why do you think?' Stony answered.

Slowly Willie came to understand. His eyes brightened with low intelligence as he looked from Stony Harte to Cameron Black.

'He is,' the woman, Emily, said, 'isn't he? He's a dead ringer for Stony.'

'Dead ringer,' Willie said with a crooked smile. He tugged involuntarily at his bent nose again.

The misgivings Cameron had felt growing mushroomed into stark fear. He knew now what they had in mind for him. He backed away half a step, but Willie moved behind him, clamped a big, broken-knuckled hand on his wrist and removed his Colt .44 from his holster, tucking it behind his belt.

Cameron tried to feign indifference, as if taking his gun was only a precaution on the outlaw's part. He tried fixing an expression of amiable unconcern on his face and suggested, 'How about if I put the horses up and rub 'em down, Stony?'

Stony didn't bother to answer. His eyes were hooded and bleak. There was no doubt in Cameron's mind now what his fate was to be. Only a pawn in a dangerous game, he would have to be sacrificed. He shrugged and half-turned as if he were part stupid. Then he bolted for the doorway. He threw a fist into Slyke's stomach, pawed at his gun which he could not recover, stumbled past Willie and was banged against the door jamb then broke free into the yard.

Cameron ducked as the first shot was fired from the cabin door, tried for the paint pony's reins and could not catch them up as the startled horse shied. Then he broke into a weaving, panicked run. Two more shots were aimed his way, missing him again.

Another bullet was loosed from one of the .44s behind him and this one did not miss. It caught him on the side of the skull like a sledge hammer, his limbs turned to rubber and Cameron Black came undone, sprawling onto his face against the cold, hard Arizona earth. One bright, volcanic light flashed through his head and then fizzled to darkness, leaving him falling into a deep, silent abyss.

*

'Good work, Pocomo,' a man was saying from out of a long, light tunnel. Someone answered in a strangely inflected voice.

'I say catch 'em, I catch 'em.' There was a pride in the words. Cameron felt a boot toe jar his ribs roughly. Someone was standing over him. Opening one eye a mere slit he saw the sun, high and white glaring down on the ranch. He closed his eyes tightly; the glare was intolerable. His head was raging with pain. There was matted blood in his hair, scabbed across one eye. He pawed at it with the web of his hand, tried to rise and fell back to the hot earth.

'Get up!' someone commanded, and Cameron was jerked to his feet by hands under his arms and at his belt.

'You sure this is him?' a third voice asked.

'It's him.'

'I track that horse thirty miles,' the man with the odd voice said. Squinting again into the terrible sunlight, Cameron saw that this one was an Indian, perhaps a Cherokee. His face was covered with white alkali dust, streaked with rivulets of sweat. 'I know that horse tracks.'

'So do I, Pocomo,' the big man answered. 'Name's "Dolly", isn't it, Stony?'

Cameron shook his head wearily. His neck seemed to have no strength. He couldn't answer, his mouth was so parched. The big man, the one who seemed to be in charge, was shaped like a barrel, with stubby legs and thick arms attached. He wore twill trousers and a faded red shirt.

There was a badge attached to his shirt front.

'Well, you ought to know,' the other man, the one who remained mounted on a black gelding, said, tilting back his hat. 'Ask him where the money is. That's all Wells Fargo wants. After that you can do with him what you like.'

'I'll ask him,' the lawman said. His voice was very ugly. He grabbed Cameron by his hair and jerked his head up, pushing him roughly against Dolly's flank. 'Come clean, Stony. It might save your life.'

'I'm not Stony Harte,' Cameron said, with a mouth that felt as if it were clogged with dust. The lawman laughed and glanced at his companions.

'See! He knew Stony's last name and no one had mentioned it.' For something to do, it seemed, more than out of anger, the sheriff bunched his big fist and drove it into Cam's ribs, forcing his breath out in a sudden rush. 'Give up the payroll, Stony. I might be able to keep you from hanging, or at least cut a few years off your sentence.'

'I'd co-operate was I you,' the man on horseback told Cameron Black. He was narrow, his face deeply tanned and lined. Apparently he was a

Wells Fargo detective from what Cam had over-heard. 'I'd hate to let Sheriff Yount loose on you. Save yourself some trouble and a lot of pain.'

'Others all ride. Fast across river,' the Indian tracker told them. 'No tracks in river. Too much sand and rocks for good sign.'

'It doesn't matter,' Sheriff Yount said, with a shrug of his heavy shoulders. 'We've got their leader now. He knows where they're bound, I guarantee you.'

'Why don't we look through the cabin again, Barney?' the Wells Fargo agent suggested.

'You do that . . . there could be a place to cache the money,' the big sheriff said, breathing roughly as he stood in front of Cameron Black, his eyes feral and cold. 'Pocomo, whyn't you see if you can't cut sign somewhere along the river? That might give us an idea where the gang is headed, though my guess is Mexico.'

'Long time gone now,' the Indian said with a small shake of his head. 'Try.'

When the other two had moved slowly away on their horses, Pocomo toward the river beyond the live oaks, and the Wells Fargo man to the cabin, the sheriff pulled a twist of tobacco from his pocket, bit off a wad of it and faced Cam deliber-ately.

'You got bad trouble, Stony.'

'I'm not—'

'No. And I'm a canary bird. Whose hat is that?' he demanded, moving his boot to nudge Stony Harte's doeskin hat with its unique silver and turquoise band. The sheriff bent down and picked it up, jamming it on Cameron Black's head. 'Fits pretty good, don't it?'

'First of all—' Cameron tried again. The sheriff would not let him speak.

'What's that gray horse's name?' he asked slyly.

'Dolly, but . . . if you'd listen to me for a minute!'

'Dolly was thirty miles south the day before yesterday, Harte. Pocomo is a tracking fool. He never lost your sign. Not only that, we have an eye-witness who saw you gun down a shotgun rider and a passenger on the Wells Fargo Tucson link. Know what else?' the large man asked, standing nearer so that his raw road scent of perspiration, stale tobacco and whiskey was rank in Cam's nostrils. 'You talk like a Georgia boy, did you know that? I spent six months down there occupying Rebel land for Sherman. I can hear Georgia all over you.'

His voice lowered. 'I don't like you Rebels. I don't like boys coming out here and raising hell, thieving and murdering. I don't like Georgia and I don't like you, Stony Harte. Understand me!' Then again, as if just for the hell of it, he slammed his fist into Cameron Black's body. The blow landed against Cam's liver and he staggered back in enormous pain, falling against Stony Harte's horse once more. Tiny multicolored sparks lit up behind his eyes and fountained away. Cameron bent double, holding himself. Dolly, tired of being abused by these man-games, tossed her head and walked away a few steps.

The Wells Fargo man had returned, leading his black horse.

'Any luck, Morton?'

'None,' the thin man answered. He removed his hat to wipe the sweat band and now Cameron saw that he was bald on the crown of his head, a monk's fringe type of baldness. He replaced the hat. 'There's no place to hide much in that shack, Barney. No floorboards, the walls are only pole and mud.' He shook his head. 'Either they buried the money nearby,' he said, scanning the brushy hillsides, 'or they rode off with it. Maybe they decided to cut Stony out of it; maybe he took that bullet graze down south and he couldn't ride.'

'They didn't bury it,' Barney Yount said definitely. 'They knew we couldn't be far behind. Besides, if they buried that scrip it would be rotted away before they could come back and retrieve it, and the silver chest would need a big hole.'

Eyes scoured Cameron Black's, hoping for some hint, perhaps. Cameron knew that the scrip

39

was already gone, that the silver had been discarded for its weight because Stony was traveling alone with one horse, and needed to travel fast and long carrying only the substantial fortune in gold, but to reveal that would be all the more damning. How could a wandering stranger be privy to these fact?

It was simple when one realized that the wandering innocent was meant to be killed and left behind as Stony, and that Harte would then be riding along a cold trail. Why hadn't Stony killed him earlier on before Cam had learned any of these things? Harte had even saved him with that snap shot which killed the rattler. Also simple when given a little thought as Stony had said, two men with arms were better than one in Apache country. And Stony had not cared to lead Cam's pony with his stiffening, rotting body strapped to it. 'Stony' had to be found as if freshly killed. The sheriff, whatever he was, was cunning enough to be able to tell a days-old body from a man who has been shot recently, apparently by his own friends in a squabble over the money.

It did no good for Cameron to know these things. He could not tell the sheriff, and the big man would not believe him at this point. The lawman's convictions had solidified and Barney Yount was an inflexible man.

'There are only two choices, Harte,' the sheriff

now said, rolling up his sleeves as the day grew oppressive with the dry heat and the shadows shortened beneath the scattered oaks. 'Give up the money and tell us where your friends went, or I'll beat you to death.'

THREE

The hulking shadow of Sheriff Yount blotted out the sun. Cameron, now seated on the hot earth, turned his hands up imploringly.

'I don't know where the money is, I tell you!' he said frantically. 'I don't know where they went.'

'Damn you, you liar,' Yount said. There was foam on his lips as he leaned down, jerked Cameron toward him by his collar and slammed a meaty fist into his face. Cameron sagged back like a flour sack, his tortured head spinning again, throbbing with pain.

Agent Morton grabbed Sheriff Yount by the arm. 'Hold on, Barney,' the slender man said. 'Maybe he really doesn't know. He took a slug off his skull. Maybe he can't remember . . . or more likely, they had already cut him out of their plans. If they tried to murder him, don't that make sense?'

'He knows, the liar!' Barney Yount said, his massive chest rising and falling with anger.

'All right,' Morton went on, still calm and logical. 'Let's say he does know and he's faking it. Where is it going to get us, Barney, if you kill him? The shape he's in it might not take much to do that. Then where would we be? Wells Fargo wants the money back, that's all – and dead men can't tell us anything.'

'No,' Barney Yount had to admit, his anger slowly cooling. He straightened up, loosened his tightly clenched fists and wiped back a strand of red hair from his forehead. 'What do you suggest we do, Morton?'

'That's your business, isn't it?'

'Yeah, I guess it is,' Yount said with a heavy sigh. 'I suppose I'll have to have his scalp sewn up and then throw him in the darkest cell Yuma prison has to offer. Ever seen that prison, Harte? A hundred and thirty degrees this time of year. Locked in a ten by ten cell. You won't like it a bit, I guarantee you. If you want to come clean now, I can transport you to Tombstone jail. It'll seem like heaven compared to the hell of Yuma. Well?' he demanded, but all Cameron Black could do was sit there and slowly, heavily wag his head.

Pocomo had returned from the river and he approached them now, shrugging. 'No good sign.

They all split apart. Maybe could catch sight four, five hours.'

'They've already got at least a twelve-hour lead on us,' Yount said, looking into the distance, 'and they have fresh ponies. We'll have to give it up, Pocomo.'

'I think so too, Sheriff.'

'But we've got *him*,' Yount said, nudging Cameron with his boot toe. 'And he'll remember after he has had his taste of Yuma prison.' The bulky lawman leaned lower, his broad shadow again covering Cameron's eyes so that he could see Yount's brutal leer. 'They say crime doesn't pay, don't they, Harte? Your friends just wanted to dust you off for your cut. Me,' he laughed, 'I'm going to help you. I'm going to put you in a nice safe place where no one but me can hurt you!'

He turned to Pocomo and said, 'Get him up onto that gray mare of his and tie his boots to the stirrups. It's going to be a long, hot ride to Yuma, boys.'

The ride was an eternity of pain beneath a blistering sun. Cameron could not sit his saddle well and they offered him water only infrequently although Yount seemed to get enjoyment out of drinking it in front of him. Sand passed under Dolly's hoofs, only sand and rock, white sand, black sand; red rock and white glittering quartz rocks. It was a forever ride across the demon desert which didn't end until he found himself thrown, half-conscious, into some underground bunker in Yuma prison.

Cameron had no memory of reaching Yuma, of being passed through the gates, of being manacled and sewn up roughly by a surgeon with hands like a tailor. The montage flitted past, out of sequence, smothered by the constant pain in his head. He slept, if it could be called that, on a broad board hung on chains from the side of the prison cell's wall. It was hot, so hot he could no longer stay in his semi-conscious world and awoke with parched lips, swollen tongue, bathed in his own sweat which the dry air quickly evaporated.

Then again it would be dark, so dark and cold that, uncovered by a blanket, he wrapped himself tightly in his arms and drew up his knees wishing for death.

The warden entered his cell after peering in through the iron-barred window cut into the heavy oaken door on what they told him was his third day in Yuma prison. A jailer with his huge ring of keys stood by silently as the little man, cheerful and neatly dressed, stood next to Cameron's bunk.

'So,' the warden said, hooking his thumbs into the pockets of his vest, 'Richard Lovelace was wrong, wasn't he?'

Cameron stared dumbly at the eager little man

in the dark suit.

'Stone walls *do* a prison make,' the man said, smiling. Apparently he was amusing himself at Cameron's expense, so Cam made no reply.

'Sit up, Mr Harte,' the warden said with an inviting gesture.

Cameron didn't bother to deny the name the warden called him by. He struggled to sit up on the plank bed, each movement causing pain to hammer in his skull. He found that his legs were in irons but his hands were free.

He had a vague memory of a great flabby, shirt-less blacksmith driving the pins into the irons while his furnace sparked and smoked. Cam touched his head and found it swathed in bandages. Then he lifted his eyes to the warden.

'I'm John Traylor, warden here. I wanted to see you, Mr Harte.'

'What is it?' Cam wanted to know.

'I like to pay all of my new wards a visit,' the man said, 'just so they know how things work here.'

'How do they work?' Cameron asked, burying his face in his palms. 'I haven't even been tried or sentenced yet, you know.'

'Mr Harte!' the warden laughed with what seemed genuine amusement. 'It's only this latest charge for which you have not had your day in court. How badly has your head been damaged?

You don't recall breaking out of the jail in Phoenix after being convicted of bank robbery and assault on a law officer! My goodness, Mr Harte, we have enough black marks in our books that it's only chance we didn't hang you the moment we saw you.'

'I didn't know,' Cameron said lamely.

'You didn't know!' Traylor drew a cigar from his coat pocket and lit it. He waved the match out slowly and smiled at Cameron. 'I guess it would be hard to remember the details of a life of crime such as you've led. Did that bullet glancing off your skull drive away all memory? If you plan to use that as a defense. . . .'

'My defense would be that I am not Stony Harte!' Cameron said so violently that the warden flinched slightly and Cam's headache began to stir angrily again.

'I see,' the warden said as if pondering this seriously. The smoke from his cigar was rank in Cameron's nostrils in this airless cell. The little man leaned closer. 'Look here, Harte, I understand you – or think I do. There's a lot of you Rebels out here. Listen, I am a Southerner myself originally, from Tennessee. But this raiding and looting has to be put to an end. The War is long over. They won. You have to live by Yankee law. It's over. This raiding of their banks, of Union Army payrolls – which by the way is the current charge

47

against you, aside from multiple murders – has to come to an end. And that man in the stage you believed to be an aggressive civilian was actually an army officer assigned to protect the soldiers' pay. That won't look good at all.' He shook his head. 'That's four capital crimes against you, and two of them Federal crimes. You haven't a chance, Harte.'

The little man stubbed out his cigar on his boot sole. His smile now was much harder. 'You might be able to wriggle free of the hanging sentences if you can convince a jury that the others in your gang did the actual killings.'

'And?' Cameron asked, noting the hesitation in the warden's voice.

'Well,' he said, flipping an open hand in a careless gesture, 'obviously returning the stolen payroll would help your cause. Fifty thousand dollars in scrip and coin is, after all, quite a bit of money, isn't it?'

It was an awful lot of money, Cameron conceded. And after the warden had gone it occurred to him through the confusion of his battered senses that most of the questioning he had been receiving was not about the crime itself, the murders, or the identity of his assumed accomplices at all.

It was all about the stolen money.

On the third morning two guards came to

remove Cameron Black from his dungeon and he was assigned work duties. The bandages had been unwound from his head and he was judged fit enough to be a part of the labor force, that being the main reason, it seemed, for the prison's existence.

Outside in the white glare of the relentless sun men could be seen breaking rocks with sledgehammers, others wheeling the rocks to their destination in wooden barrows, their movements stiff and unnatural due to their leg irons.

The rocks were intended to be used to lay a bed for the Eastern Arizona Railroad's path across the relentless shifting sand of the desert. Cameron doubted such a project could ever be completed. His knowledge of the desert left him convinced that the implacable desert and its uncertain foundation would defy such a project forever.

Nonetheless, men worked on. If they fell out it was of no importance to the prison officials, others could be found to take their place. Most of these prisoners were young, arrested for minor crimes such as brawling or drunkenness. They labored on for twelve hours a day, winter or summer, their hands and faces growing dark and then nearly blackened by the desert sun until eventually the dead skin began to rot and peel away, leaving them with gaping patches of new raw flesh which would become savagely blistered.

There were other jobs at the prison. Those engaged in work in the tomb of the prison entrails were chalk gray with the ghostly pallor of men who never saw the sunlight at all, but only suffered in its unendurable heat. Cameron discovered early on that there was no doubt about which gang men belonged to because of this difference. Inside laborers, like gaunt skeletons, colorless and thin because of the reduced rations they were given to survive on, contrasted sharply with the sun-blistered, heavy-shouldered laborers on the rock pile.

Cameron Black was assigned to the boot shop.

'What are they saving you for?' his first acquaintance there, a Dutchman named Voorman asked.

'What do you mean?'

'The inside jobs are only given to those they want to keep alive. For trial, for political favors.'

'I don't know,' Cameron told the Dutchman. But he did know, of course. *They wanted to keep him alive until he would give up the gold* – gold he didn't have.

There was no short supply of boots to work on – old boots. Cameron never saw a new pair in his time there. Only old ones, needing restitching, new soles and a cursory shine. These were removed, a pair at a time from those who died on the rockpile. There were hundreds of them needing repair they never got while their last owner was alive.

'Dead men don't need boots,' the Dutchman said as he tossed another dusty, broken pair on the huge pile in the back of the boot shop. No man out of Yuma prison was ever buried with his boots on.

The gruel became thinner now that Cameron was on the mend. It was of oats in tepid water. The roaches who had stupidly crawled into the cooking pots or come bagged with the oats were the only additional ingredients, although once Cameron did drop his bowl of oatmeal when a still very alive centipede made its way up out of the gray lumpy gruel to crawl over the rim.

He did not eat the next day, but that was self-defeating and he learned to eat whatever was served with his eyes closed, his nostrils pinched. It made him long for the days past and Stony Harte's stringy, flavorless Indian pemmican.

That and the clear flavor of free air. Life!

He hadn't forgotten Stony Harte. The man had betrayed his friendship, had tried to murder him, had left Cam to rot in this prison. No, Cameron Black had not forgotten.

On the morning of his twelfth day in prison, before the sun had truly risen and the cell's interior was cold enough to freeze a man to the bone, his door was kicked open and Sheriff Barney Yount, accompanied by two blue-uniformed guards, was admitted. Cameron sat up sharply on his rough plank bunk.

'Hello, Stony,' Yount said.

'Sheriff,' Cam answered warily.

'They tell me you're better now.'

'Some,' Cameron replied.

'That's fine,' the big sheriff responded. 'Well enough to stand up to the beating I promised you?'

'Listen, that's—'

As usual, Cameron was unable to get past his first few words with the sadistic lawman. Yount bulked large in the pre-dawn gray; the two guards turned their backs as the sheriff waded in with both fists clenched, his small mouth tight with glee. Cameron couldn't have fought off the giant lawman before, now with his weight down, his muscles thinning, he had no chance at all. He was as a child before the brutish lawman's onslaught.

There is no need to describe the brutality of the beating. Cameron himself could hardly remember enough after the first blow to tell it. He was like a schoolboy being pummeled by a heavyweight fighter, fist after fist landing on any exposed portion of his body. His mouth filled with hot scarlet blood behind loosened teeth. He heard the grunting of the sheriff accompanying every blow as he savaged Cameron's body with asking the same questions with each pile-driver strike.

'Where is it? Do I have to kill you, Harte?'

It was only over when Cameron lost consciousness and couldn't even attempt an answer. He woke sometime around midnight, by rough reckoning, and dragged himself toward his bunk. Conceding that his bunk was no softer than the stone floor of the prison, unable to drag himself upright on battered limbs, he sagged back to the floor, not sleeping but mewling the night away in despair.

They did not come to roust him out to his work in the boot shop the next morning. The door opened only once as he lay curled against the floor and a bowl of the thin gruel was placed near him by one of the guards. Cameron thought he saw a faint flicker of sympathy in the man's eyes, but that was little consolation.

My life has ended, he thought as he clawed nearer the gruel. They'll never let me out of here unless I tell them, but I can't tell them what I don't know! The spoon in his hand seemed too heavy and slippery to lift and he fell down, rolling over onto his back to stare at the colorless stone ceiling, cursing the soul of the treacherous Stony Harte.

It was daylight again when the door opened next and Cameron cowered in a corner like a beaten hound, his arms across his face. But no hand was placed upon him. The heavy door opened and then clanged shut again. He heard shuffling steps in the cell and finally opened an eye to watch the lean, long-jawed, mustached man in prison gray lowering the other bunk on its chains. The new prisoner sat on it, testing the chains with his weight and studied Cameron.

'They giving you a rough time of it?' the new prisoner asked.

'That's not the half of it,' Cam answered past battered ribs and bruised lips.

'It's a rough hole we're in, brother,' the mustached man said. He didn't move, but continued to watch Cameron Black. The newcomer stretched his arms once and then clasped his hands together between his knees. 'Want some help up?'

Ashamed, Cameron nodded heavily and the stranger got to his feet, hooking his hands under Cameron's armpits, lifting him to wobbly legs and guiding him toward his bunk where Cameron settled with a moan. He sat there, his head hanging as if weighted by an anvil.

'What'd you do to get them so mad at you?' the new prisoner asked.

'Trusted the wrong man,' Cam answered. True to the prisoner's code, the new man did not ask him what his crime had been, but only nodded.

'They just brought me up from Phoenix. I've got another trial coming Monday,' Cameron's cell mate said despondently. 'I'm pretty sure they're going to hang me. Me, I trusted the wrong woman, and now, brother, I am going to pay for that.'

Cameron remained in a seated position, his back against the wall behind his plank bunk. He was afraid that if he lay down he might never get up again. He could not sleep, nor did he want to. It would take more than a few more hours of unconsciousness to revive his battered body.

'My name's Elliott Hogan,' the new man said, reaching out a hand toward Cameron. Cam took it weakly and nodded a bare inch in acknowledgement.

'Cameron Black.'

'Glad to meet you. Sorry it had to be in here,' Hogan said.

'Is there any place left but here?' Cameron murmured through his puffed lips.

'Feel like talking? It seems you probably don't.'

'It makes no difference,' Cam answered, with a one-shouldered shrug.

'It can all be told another time,' Hogan said indifferently. 'You know how it is – a wronged man feels like talking about his troubles, and brother that's what I am: a wronged man. I've got the feeling that maybe you are too.' He leaned nearer out of the heated darkness of the prison shadows. 'You listen to me and think over what I say, Black.' His voice dropped to a hoarse whisper. 'Because I think that I can find a way for the two of us to break our shackles and free ourselves from this hellhole. If you're willing to throw in with me.'

A faint hope flickered within Cameron's heart. He stared at Elliot Hogan, doubting that he could have heard what he thought he did.

'Are you kidding me, Hogan?'

'Not at all, pal. Listen to what I have to say. It takes two men to work my plan. Throw in with me and we have a chance, Cameron. In here,' he said, looking around the cell before returning to Cameron Black's battered face, 'neither of us has a chance in hell of getting out alive.'

FOUR

'The man's as dumb as dirt,' Elliot Hogan said, tilting back in the wooden chair in Warden Traylor's office. He was contentedly smoking a cigar the warden had given him after he had been escorted there by two tough-looking guards. Sheriff Yount stood near the open window of the warden's office, staring out across the white expanse of endless desert. The Wells Fargo agent, Morton, sat in a chair identical to Hogan's, holding his hat loosely between his legs.

'I doubt that,' Morton said, without lifting his eyes to the mustached guard in prison garb, which Hogan actually was. 'A man who's pulled off as many successful robberies and escaped as frequently as Stony Harte can hardly be considered stupid.'

'He swallowed my whole story, the whole plan,' Elliot Hogan insisted. He had been tilted back on

57

his chair. Now he let the front legs drop to the granite floor with a bang. It was a challenging gesture.

'Or so he is letting you believe!' Morton said quietly, but with emphasis, rubbing at the bald spot on the crown of his head.

'What are you getting at, Morton?' Sheriff Yount asked without turning from the window.

'I'm just saying that in my estimation it's a mistake to let a man as dangerous as Stony Harte pass out of the prison walls.'

Warden Traylor asked softly, 'Have you a better idea on how we can recover the money – find the rest of this murderous gang?' He went on, 'God knows we've tried everything, beating him half to death. . . .' He cast a quick, sharp glance at the sheriff's bearish back. 'It's your company, after all that's going to pay the price if the money from the hold-up isn't found, Morton.'

'And you who will lose out on the reward – a third of the loot.'

'Would Wells Fargo rather have two-thirds of the money back and the gang hanged, or nothing!' Warden Traylor said with a sharpness that was uncharacteristic. 'And the army, sir! This represents a large loss to the army. They would be understandably reluctant to ship future payrolls with Wells Fargo. They would be more likely to return to the old method—'

'A much more expensive method,' Morton interrupted.

'More expensive but surer method of transporting it protected by their own armed troops.'

Morton made no answer. He stared at the floor of the warden's office. Slowly the sun was lifting above the eastern horizon. Scarlet tendrils streaked the grayness. It would soon be as hot as Hades again.

'Tell me again how the plan is to work,' Morton said, with a heavy sigh. He liked none of this, but if the payroll was not recovered, nor the Harte gang caught, he might as well resign and return to his father's farm in Indiana. He would never be trusted in such a responsible position again. Wells Fargo did not like to lose money. More, they would not accept losing face at the hands of a gang of outlaws. Ever.

Morton was under no illusions as to the kind of men he was dealing with here. They wanted the reward – a third of the $50,000 dollars which they would split among themselves. A tidy amount. Who else was there to turn to on this fringe of the frontier? No one at all.

'All right,' Morton said finally. 'Tell me again about the plan.'

'I'm going to grease him for a few more days, maybe a week,' Hogan said eagerly. 'I mean, this is all happening pretty fast for Harte. Maybe he won't bite at first if he thinks it's a set-up. He could be thinking that, after all. I'll keep feeding him my story, a little at a time.

'Meanwhile he needs to be given more reason to grow desperate. Until he's wild with the need to break free. You see what I mean?' Hogan said with a wink. 'So that's he's willing to chance anything rather than stay here.'

'Beatings?' Morton asked with distaste.

'Oh, hell no,' Hogan replied. 'We've to let him get healthier so he'll feel he's up to a break and a dash across the desert. Right now he couldn't whip a kitten, and he knows it. No,' Hogan said, in a low, brutal voice, 'we've got to find a way to let his body grow stronger while we gut him of his soul.'

Warden John Traylor nodded. He knew exactly what his confederate had in mind. They had already discussed it in private. There had been no need to let this two-bit animal of a sheriff or the Wells Fargo agent in on it. It was the warden's play to make. He had all the cards. He had Stony Harte under his legal detention and control.

Besides, this was hardly the first time he and Officer Hogan had played this sort of game. Over the years they had made no small amount of money doing just what they planned now. Help a prisoner escape. Send him into the desert with a 'trusted' friend and then pull a gun on him.

Sometimes it worked and the escaped prisoner would be willing – eager – to trade his freedom for his hidden ill-gotten gains.

Sometimes it did not work so smoothly. There were bodies scattered beneath the wild desert sands that no man would ever find. Just more victims of Yuma prison.

'We have to give it a try,' Morton said. 'Let's just hope that Harte is as beaten down as you believe – and as stupid as Hogan seems to think.'

Cameron Black was hardly as stupid as Hogan seemed to believe. He had, since the moment the scoundrel had been placed in the cell with him, considered the possibility that the man was an informer, a prisoner placed with him to prod, pry and wait for secrets to be divulged. Cameron had never been in prison before, but native intelligence warned him. Then, too, Voorman in the bootshop had whispered over the clatter of stitching machines, 'They've tried beating you, Harte. Watch out next for the devious touch.'

Voorman had taken Cameron under his wing since he had returned battered and stiff, swollen and disfigured, to the shop. The old, wiser Dutchman had seen all the tricks the prison had to offer before this.

'I'll be careful, thanks, Voorman,' Cameron Black told him. One thought, occurring to him as he spent a cramped, exhausted night on his bunk with the glow of the half moon sketching a barred rectangle on the floor of his cell, was that it in no way helped his chances of escaping to continue to deny being Stony Harte. It was Harte, after all, that they wanted to escape to lead them to his stash of loot – or so Cameron now believed.

In what he pretended was a secret midnight conversation with his cell mate, he told Elliot Hogan, 'Sure I told them my name was Cameron Black. I made that up out of thin air. I thought that they might believe they had the wrong man. It didn't work. They knew all along who I was.'

'Harte?' Hogan asked drowsily from his bunk. His back was to Cameron, but his eyes were bright with the glow of success.

'Sure,' Cam said. 'But it didn't help any. I'm doomed, Hogan. They'll hang me sure unless you really have a way to escape.'

'Trust me,' was all Hogan said, and the traitor went to sleep easily.

Cameron did not sleep, could not. The pain still lay upon him heavily. Even if escape were possible, what then? Would he find himself riding the wasteland with a thug like Elliot Hogan who would learn the truth soon enough, that Cam had no idea where the stolen money might be hidden? If Hogan did not shoot him dead, what then? Was Cameron to attempt to find the real Stony Harte in all that desert vastness and face down the feared gunfighter and his entire gang? There was no way out of this tangled hell, no road to freedom.

The next move the penitentiary powers made was more devious and savage than any outright beating. It was insidious and macabre.

Cameron had not seen the short, one-eyed guard with the fantastic broom of red beard before, but one morning the man spoke to Voorman, crossed the shop and found Cameron at his stitching machine. He place a meaty hand on Cameron's shoulder.

'You'll be here awhile,' the man said, his one good eye cold and black and cloudy. 'They want you to learn the whole job.'

'What do you mean?' Cameron asked, wiping his hands on his shabby blue apron.

'Every man assigned to boot shop takes a turn.' At Cameron's still-confused expression, the guard added, 'It's about learning where the boots you work on come from.'

Voorman watched with his head down, unspeaking as the guard removed Cameron from the shop. They walked across the inner yard, a square of white earth enclosed on all sides by high walls. Then, with another sign to a guard posted high above them, the two men passed through a double oaken door twelve feet in height. Beyond these stood a heavy wagon with huge steel-tired wheels. The guard nudged Cameron toward the tailgate, poking his back with a baton. Already Cameron knew by the odor rising from the wagon what to expect. He tried to turn away, but there was no choice. Dead prisoners, stacked carelessly in the back three deep awaited him.

'Get those boots off, Harte,' the guard ordered him. 'Here's the gunny sacks to put them in.'

Cameron climbed into the bed of the wagon and, moving among the faceless dead, he got to work, untying their boots. Beyond him he could see a burial crew waiting patiently like gray-uniformed buzzards. Three ancient-looking men from the prison laundry also waited to retrieve the dead men's uniforms so that they could be repaired and washed for the next to arrive.

At first Cameron moved gingerly, out of sheer horror, keeping his eyes always averted from the faces of the dead. Later he moved with incautious fury, ripping the shabby boots from the feet of the prisoners, needing only to be finished with the repugnant task.

Broiling under the incessant heat of the monitoring sun he shoved and dug and worked madly among them, his fingers unlacing the toughest knots with savage strength. Finished, he leapt from the wagon, was momentarily sick and began at the guard's instructions to shove the boots into the burlap bags provided, as the body strippers from the laundry moved in like a horde of scavenger birds.

'You'll get used to it,' the guard told Cameron. 'Over time.'

Shouldering his grisly trophies, Cameron trudged back through the gate and walked blindly across the sand of the courtyard to the steel rear door of the boot shop, held open by a grim-faced Voorman.

They said he would get used to it, but he would not! It was a sickening, disgusting scene which he only got through by pretending he was someone else, far distant, performing an unimaginable task in some underworld nightmare. He thought he had suffered too much, that he was too tough now to be affected, but when he fell asleep it was only after lying awake for long hours sobbing. Elliot Hogan spoke to him only briefly, and Cameron was glad for that.

The next morning he walked to the boot shop like one of the dead himself. Voorman's pale eyes were on him as Cam shakily started his stitching machine and picked up the first pair of boots he had to repair. Voorman moved beside him, pretending to oil the spindle of the machine.

'Is it tonight then?' the Dutchman asked.

'What!' Cameron was thoroughly startled.

'What do you mean, Voorman?'

The Dutchman nodded toward Cameron's ankles. 'They've removed your chains.'

'Yes, early this morning. So that I could clamber more easily in and out of the wagons, they said.'

'Don't you believe that,' Voorman said, glancing around to see that there were no guards nearby. 'You'll be making your break soon. Tonight is my guess.'

'No.'

'Yes, Cam. They're sure they've got you ready to make even a reckless attempt now and, mark my words, Hogan will have a plan to put before you.'

'He already has,' Cam said in a low voice. 'At least a part of it.'

'And you'll agree to try it,' the Dutchman said.

'I have to, Voorman! What choice do I have? Except to leave here without my own boots.'

'None at all.' Voorman set down the oil can and pretended to be examining the leather drive belt on the machine. 'But once they find out you don't know where the money is . . . what then?'

'I don't know,' Cam said wearily.

'Out on the desert alone. They'll plug you and leave you. You know that, don't you?'

'I guess I have no choice. It might be a cleaner death than what they have in store for me here.'

'You're right,' Voorman said, straightening up.

'There's no choice. This is all rigged, Cam. You guessed it; I *know* it. I've seen it before.' His voice dropped to a whisper. 'I can offer you some insurance.'

'What do you mean?' Cam asked, his eyes intent on his sewing, the waxed thread spinning on the revolving spindle, as a slow-walking guard patrolled the perimeter of the boot shop.

'Take me with you,' Voorman pleaded. His grip was tight on Cam's arm. 'I can watch your back; I can be of help.'

'Hogan won't let you go with us.'

'Damn Hogan! He'll have no choice. Don't you see! You'll just tell him that so long as you were making a break for it, you asked me along, too.' Voorman's eyes were frantic now. 'He won't dare complain. Would a *real* convict turn his back on one of his brothers?'

'It won't work.'

'It will,' Voorman insisted. His voice grew uglier. 'I got to get out, Cam, don't you see? If you don't take me I'll scream loud and long so that the warden won't dare let you break out. And then,' he promised darkly, 'when I have you back inside, in my shop, I'll make your life sheer living hell for as long as you are locked up. Which, I don't have to remind you, will be for life.'

Cameron couldn't tell if it was viciousness or desperation that caused the man he thought to be his only friend in the prison to talk this way, but Voorman's motive didn't matter. Only the plan mattered. And Hogan's plan was bound to succeed because, as both men knew full well by now, the breakout was a set-up. Cameron nodded very slowly.

'I'll talk to Hogan—'

'Don't! Just find out how he's planned it out. I don't want the warden learning anything – we both know Hogan is an informer. Just give me a crack at an open door, Cameron.' Voorman looked briefly ashamed. 'If I bullied you, I'm sorry. I do not wish to die here, no more than you do. A man gets to be like a caged animal the longer he's caged. I'll go with you and I'll be your right hand as long as you need me.'

It was hard not to believe Voorman; it was diffi-cult not to trust his word. Cameron knew the man's background. He was formerly a butcher in Phoenix. His wife and her lover had had the misfortune of being caught in an unfortunate situation when Voorman had arrived home early from work after a shipment of hogs had been delayed. Younger then, hot-blooded, Voorman had addressed the two with a cleaver.

Voorman was awaiting execution, but he had never worn leg irons and was given cornbread and slivers of salt pork, even an occasional piece of fruit among other things beyond the usual prison fare because he was classified as a 'special circumstance' prisoner – the circumstance being that his brother was a member of the Territorial Assembly. The brother's term was nearly up; the next election was much in doubt. The Dutchman's fate hung on the scales of politics. The prison commission was not corrupt enough to grant a murderer outright release, but it had been willing to bide its time regarding the execution of an assemblyman's brother. After all Voorman was not going anywhere anyway.

But Voorman was one more of the walking dead inhabiting the prison. A stroke of the warden's pen could send any one of them to the scaffold at sunrise. 'Stony Harte' included.

Any possibility of escape was preferable to living beneath the shadow of the hangman's noose.

FIVE

It was not on that night nor the one after that the escape was attempted, but on the third night.

Without Elliot Hogan's knowledge, Cameron had laid it open to Voorman. The Dutchman listened thoughtfully and then commented, 'Well, it is a set-up then. That's certain.'

'What makes you so sure?' Cam asked.

'Tell me again the short of it,' Voorman prompted.

'According to Hogan there's only a single window in the entire prison that has no bars on the window: the window in the warden's office. I've never seen it myself.'

'I have,' Voorman said. 'That's true enough. But that office is beyond a steel door.'

'Hogan is the janitor in that wing, as you know. He says he has found a way to wedge the door. A lock will seem to secure the door, but it will be just slightly ajar.'

'He says that, does he?' Voorman said doubtfully.

'He says that. Maybe he's wrong. But we all know there's risk involved. We could get trapped in the corridor and caught again. For myself, it's worth any risk. What can they do to me that they haven't already done or threatened?'

'True enough.' Voorman again grew meditative. 'I can manage to slip up into the corridor. It's easy enough. But once we're out the warden's window, what then?'

'Hogan's bribed a man from the stable to bring two horses up outside the western wall.'

'Bribed with what?' Voorman asked skeptically.

'I'm not sure. Hogan said it wasn't important for me to know.'

'It's a set-up for sure,' Voorman repeated. 'And there's nothing wrong with that. You see, Cam, there's no risk involved at all. The warden's plotted it. He and Hogan. They want you to lead them to the loot from the robbery. They're making it all quite simple. Hogan just has to keep telling you that it is really dangerous to convince you that you must go along. To continue to place it in your mind that you're willing to risk all for freedom.'

'And I am,' Cam admitted. 'Plot or not, I'm going.'

The way Voorman put it, Cameron could understand that he might be about to be taken for a ride. No matter, that was the chance he had to take. He couldn't do another month in Yuma prison, let alone years, a lifetime. This could be his only chance at escape – ever.

Voorman said, 'Just be sure not to breathe a word about me. I'm going along, Cam. And I'm on your side.'

Was *that* even true, Cameron wondered as he returned to his work? Maybe it was Voorman who was the informer and Cam had been duped into telling him the plan. Maybe it was Voorman who was reporting to the warden and taking a hand in the break for his own reasons. What reasons? Maybe his brother still had influence with the warden. Maybe his politically connected brother had manipulated Warden Traylor, bribed him to let the big-shouldered Dutchman escape.

In the night these thoughts spun and collided with each other in Cameron's mind which he had to admit was even now not as clear as it should be after the bullet that had grooved his scalp, the beatings he had endured, the starvation and barbaric treatment he had endured.

None of his suspicions mattered; now all that he cared about was escaping this rotting, oppressive prison. He would rather take his chances on the open desert with two convicted criminals than spend another night on that rough plank bunk with the rats scuttling from hole to hole, with his stomach knotting with hunger. A man should at least die free if he must die.

Cameron vowed to trust neither of them – as he had once trusted Stony Harte to his sorrow. It was Yuma prison or the long sand desert. Both savage wastes in their own way, but he had made his choice. He was going to make the escape no matter what was to come.

Cameron Black had been asleep for no more than an hour when he felt the presence of Elliot Hogan next to him and heard him whisper from the darkness.

'Up now. Quiet and cautious, son. We're going over the wall.'

Rubbing roughly at his eyes, Cameron sat up on his bunk. 'How. . . ?' he mumbled.

'Shut up and do as I say,' Elliot Hogan hissed. 'This is our only chance.'

Cameron listened to the instructions whispered into his ear. Incredulous, but desperate – they had indeed managed to make him the most desperate of men – he agreed.

'The guard won't fall for it,' he had to object.

'For you he will. The warden can't let Stony Harte die until they have the money. Everybody knows what kind of shape you're in! Just do it!'

The plan was a simple one, of the kind they worked out in dime novels. He lay back on his bunk, moaning as loudly and pitiably as he could. Elliot went to the door and began calling for the night guard who approached on heavy feet.

'What is it, Hogan?'

'What do you think, you fool? Harte's dying. That sheriff broke him up real good. He won't last in here. You've got to get him to the doc's.'

The guard hesitated only a minute then drew the set of keys from his belt to open the heavy door. Elliot Hogan stood behind the door as it opened and, as the guard entered the room to stride toward 'Stony Harte', Hogan stepped up behind him and slammed his joined fists into the base of the prison guard's skull. The man dropped to the floor.

The fix is in, Cameron thought, as Hogan urged him to his feet.

If he had had any doubts before, Cameron had none now. No trained guard would enter the cell alone. He would have summoned help. Hogan had hit the man hard, but that hard? No. The man had fallen softly, not like a felled tree. The fix is in, and somehow that raised Cameron's morale. They wanted him to escape the prison. He wanted nothing more himself. Let the future take care of itself.

'Come on,' Hogan whispered fiercely. Cameron stepped around the fallen guard's body and followed Hogan into the corridor. No other guard was in sight. Cameron smiled again. It was a game they were playing and he was beginning to like it very much. He tried to act stupid and concerned, moving tentatively as Hogan swiftly followed the corridor toward the stairs leading down to the warden's office.

'Hurry up!'

'Where are the guards?'

'At a meeting: I told you I had a reason for picking this night,' Hogan lied thinly.

Cameron almost laughed out loud. Let him lie, let him complete the ruse. In only a little time he would be free on the desert. Then let Hogan and the others do their best; he would at least have a chance.

They clattered down the adobe steps, their heavy work boots making far too much noise. Still no one else stirred in the prison until they had nearly reached the steel door to the warden's office. The figure appeared from out of the shadows. Hogan drew up short, obviously confused and startled.

'I'm going with you boys,' Voonman said in a low voice.

'The hell you are,' Hogan said bitterly.

'The hell I'm not,' Voorman said, and, in his hand, Cameron could make out the long, thin menace of a leather awl. 'No time for arguing now, Hogan.'

'No,' Hogan agreed haltingly. He knew that Voorman was a killer and believed the man would use the long deadly awl if pushed to it.

'Get the door,' Voorman commanded, and Hogan did so, cursing under his breath. He shot a poisonous glance at Cameron, knowing who had given up the plan to Voorman. Cameron Black cared nothing at all for the threat or Hogan's frustration. The three men shouldered through the partially locked steel door and made for the window opposite. They quickly dragged the warden's desk beneath the high narrow window and in another moment were outside.

It was a matter of minutes before they had scaled the twelve-foot outer wall using the Indian ladder made from a barked pole with a dozen cross pieces secured to it with rawhide. Then, dropping to the sandy earth on the far side, Hogan led them on a weaving run through the tall sage and greasewood to a small clearing where two horses waited in the night, their eyes bright with curiosity and reflected starlight.

'There's only two horses,' Hogan said, stating the obvious.

'They'll do to get us on our way,' Voorman said. 'I'll ride behind you, Hogan.'

'Why not with Stony?' Hogan said complainingly.

'Because I say we do it this way,' Voorman said, and Hogan, knowing what the desperate man could do with a thrust of the awl, could only nod with resignation.

Cameron took one of the horses, a roan with a bad coat, while the other men clambered aboard a time-weary bay, an old army horse, Cameron guessed. Neither was in its prime, but why would the escapees be supplied with sturdy mounts? Cameron wished he had Dolly under him. He might even then have made a break for it if he had Harte's mare, but he did not. He followed docilely. From here on, he knew, every chance at escape had to be attanded to.

There was a small creek here which was the prison's water supply. As usual in this part of the country it was lined with willow brush, here and there a clump of cottonwood trees casting shadows against the sand and only now and then a sycamore. They followed the creek northward for half a mile and then Voorman had Hogan halt the bay horse.

'Back toward the south now, I think.'

'We're wasting time!' Hogan said peevishly.

'It's not time wasted if we can confuse them,' Voorman said strongly. 'Once we hit the flats we're visible for miles and any good horses can run down these pieces of dog meat we're riding. I don't intend to get caught, do you, Hogan?'

'Of course not,' Hogan said indignantly. He wiped his hand across his face. The moon was beginning to rise too quickly to the west. 'I just wanted to put some ground under us before they got wise.'

There was palpable tension between the two, each mistrusting the other as they started to backtrack, riding in the creek proper to disguise their tracks. Hopefully the prison did not have an Indian tracker or an experienced army scout at its disposal. Most men, Cameron knew, could not find such slight traces as a stone chipped by a steel horseshoe, let alone follow after them swiftly. Voorman, he knew, was correct and he was momentarily glad that the Dutchman was with him.

But which of the two was to be more feared? Hogan's job was to find the missing stolen money by coercing Cameron Black. Once he finally came to understand that Cameron was not Stony Harte, he was apt simply to leave him in the desert to die. Voorman? Did the Dutchman simply wish to escape or had he made a separate bargain with the authorities to try to make them reconsider his own pending death sentence?

There was no telling. Cameron could trust neither of them, he knew. His wish had been to find Stony Harte, somehow recover the loot and return it. Return it to . . . he was still a young man and unused to duplicity, but he realized that Warden Traylor and Sheriff Barney Yount who had been at this sort of business for a long time would happily welcome him back with the money – and as happily toss him back into a cell where he would never live to tell his tale.

No, the only intelligent thing to do, he considered, as his horse plodded on along the dwindling watercourse and they moved out onto the wide desert, was to wait for his chance and make a break for California, Mexico . . . anywhere.

But that would leave Stony Harte unpunished, wouldn't it? And for what Stony's betrayal had caused him to go through, the bandit would pay if Cameron could find a way.

'Where'd you get these horses?' Voorman demanded angrily.

'When you're in need you can't pick and choose,' Hogan shot back, regaining his reckless-ness.

'This damn' beast is staggering already. We're going to have to walk a way and we haven't made twenty miles. And look at that half-moon rising! We're nothing but targets out here.'

'If you hadn't doubled back. . . .' Hogan sput-tered.

'If we hadn't, they'd probably already have us!'

The argument was somewhat surreal since both men knew that there would be no posse swooping down on them until they had somehow convinced or forced Cameron to show them where the stolen money was hidden. But both men were on edge – Cameron thought Hogan was nervous because he did not want to leave the pursuit behind and feared the doubling back might have done so. Then Voorman, although he probably would have liked to see the money, was a convicted killer who feared the men from the prison could be too close.

Cam allowed them their squabble, pretending to know nothing. Nonetheless, the horses, aged and out of condition, were weary and the three swung down to walk, leading the ponies across the moon-glossed white desert. The second day was a duplicate of the first, horse and man staggering across an endless desert waste with a merciless sun overhead.

'We got to make camp,' Hogan complained, as they struggled on through the deep sand.

'Not out here,' Voorman said. 'Let's find us a place to lay up after sunrise. If we can't find water, we won't make it far in the heat.'

'If we could find a ranch, maybe a small pueblo where we could snag up some good horses. . . .'

' "If" is a fine and meaningless word,' Voorman grumbled.

'Hell with you,' Hogan said. He was gradually regaining his truculence, convinced now, perhaps, that Voorman wasn't going to attempt to murder him.

The sand became deeper and by the middle of the night they found themselves wandering through a moonscape of dunes, forty- to fifty-feet high. The horses labored on, Cameron could hear their breathing and the hard breathing of the men. Hogan, Cameron noticed, looked back across his shoulder more and more frequently as if waiting for help to arrive. It was still far too soon; and then, maybe Voorman's maneuvering back on the creek had truly concealed their course from any pursuers.

'There's no two ways about it,' Hogan said, as the three men sat resting in the scant shade of a half-dozen ocotillo bushes. The spiny plants rose twenty feet over their heads and the tips of these 'coachman's whips' were decorated with incarnadine flowers at this time of year. The shadows of the tall whiplike plants wove and recrossed casting a basket weave of shadow against the hot sand. Cameron saw a fat horned toad, body panting as it breathed the hot dusty air.

'We've got to find a little town, a ranch.'

'Water,' Voorman said.

'Yes. At least water, or we're not long for it. How about it, Harte? They say you know this desert as well as any man.'

Cameron hesitated a moment too long before answering, 'Not this far south, I'm afraid.'

'Water, boys,' Voorman repeated. 'Some clothes if we can find them,' he said, plucking at his pale, ill-fitting prison garb. 'And fresh horses. We haven't got a chance continuing as we are.'

They weren't quite desperate yet, but as twilight again began to dull the land with deep violet, Cameron's lips were cracked with the heat and the back of his neck was burned raw. The two horses – what were they, plow horses! – stumbled on through the sand and then across the rock-strewn flats with their heads lowered, bodies swaying without energy. All the same, the horses were liable to last longer than they were out here. One more day – did they have the strength to ride one more day through the desert's blast-furnace heat?

'If we could find the Colorado, we'd be all right,' Voorman said.

'That's a big snaking river. Which direction is it from here, do you think, Dutchman?'

'I don't know! Damn all.'

'We'll be all right. It will take some time, that's all,' Hogan said, with a confidence he might or might not have felt. 'No one said it would be easy. We all knew what we were up against when we made this choice.'

After sundown on this night they camped on a low, rocky rise where yucca and some thorny mesquite trees grew. No one spoke. They were all thirsty, all hungry. Tempers were too short to risk much conversation.

Voorman did say, as he stood and pointed out toward the south, 'Boys, I believe I see light that way. Camp-fire maybe, maybe a town!'

Neither of the others could see it; besides, whatever it was, it was too far for them to investigate on that cold night with man and horse beaten by the long miles.

'I say we strike out that direction come morning,' the Dutchman said. 'I tell you, I saw light.'

'It makes no difference to me,' Hogan said, as he rolled up in his only blanket. Although Cameron knew that it probably did. Each day was taking them away from where the money was supposed to be hidden. Both of his companions had to be aware of that.

Nearly asleep, Cameron was awakened by a shuffling sound near his poor bed. He saw the Dutchman hovering over him and he stiffened reflexively. Voorman bent low and whispered very low but excitedly.

'Hogan's got to have a gun with him. I mean to get it when he's full asleep. Are you with me, Harte?'

He nodded slowly. Voorman clapped him on the shoulder and skulked away. Cameron Black was still a cub among these violent wolves. He should have considered before that Hogan would have a gun. Of course he would, perhaps hidden in his saddle-bags. How else could he have been sure of gaining the upper hand when the time came?

He hadn't meant to agree to Voorman's plan, but there had been no choice. To join Voorman would incur Hogan's wrath, but to refuse the Dutchman would raise the suspicions of both of them as to where his loyalties lay.

The die was now cast for the attempt anyway. Cameron rested on his back, squirming from time to time as the rocks prodded him. He had one hand behind his head and, as he lay there in the silence, the dark near shadow of a great horned owl cast its sudden broad-winged silhouette against the rising half moon and it sent a little tremor down his spine.

Had he believed in omens as ancient men had. . . . He needed no omen to tell him that this night could come to no good end.

Voorman touched his shoulder and beckoned and Cameron rose to his knees. Silently then they inched to where Hogan lay curled up on his side. The men moved slowly and silently, on hands and knees across the cold camp. Hogan groaned in his sleep and rolled over toward them. His eyes opened slightly, and Cameron could see the white glow in the mask of the mustached man's dark face.

Cameron saw Voorman leap forward and he tried to hold him, but there was nothing he could do to stop it. Hogan threw up protective arms but the heavy stone in the Dutchman's hand was already arcing down. It struck Hogan solidly on the skull and Hogan sagged back lifelessly.

Voorman turned and sat on the ground, grinning.

'Don't look like that, Stony. You know he would have made you lead him to the loot and then he would have watched as you dug your own grave.' He rose heavily with a grunt of effort. 'I told you I'd be your right hand.' He nodded at the inert form of Hogan as if that were proof of his statement. 'Now let's find that gun.'

About that, Voorman proved to be correct. The gun was not hidden away in the saddle-bags of Hogan's horse, however. They found it strapped to his leg just above the ankle. Voorman opened the cylinder gate, satisfied himself that the revolver was fully loaded and nodded.

'We're half again as well off,' he said, tucking the pistol behind his belt. 'Two horses, two men – and no one we have to watch behind our backs.'

Cameron nodded. His stomach was cramped with revulsion. He liked none of this, had not from the start. At the first possibility, he was going to make an attempt to escape.

Voorman was standing, hands on his hips, looking again toward the south where he thought he had seen lights earlier. He glanced up at the bright half-moon, still and silver hanging above them and told Cameron, 'We might as well be traveling. I think there's plenty of moonlight. Besides,' he said disparagingly, 'I've had enough of him to last me.'

So had Cameron. He kept his eyes averted from the formless figure sprawled against the ground as he saddled and mounted up, riding the roan once again. The horse allowed his weight as if with utmost sadness, but with stolid resignation. They rode slowly southward. The terrain rolled gently, but the multitude of rocks strewn across the barren hills made for slow going. There were a few flowering yuccas around and now and then a patch of evil-looking cholla, 'jumping cactus', their barbed spines silver in the moonlight.

Cameron still could see no lights on the far horizon hours later when Voorman suddenly drew up and, holding the bay's reins loosely between two fingers enquired with some irritation, 'You *ain't* really Stony Harte, are you?'

'No,' Cam said. 'I told you.'

'You told it both ways,' the Dutchman reminded him

'I'm not Harte.'

'I didn't think so. And then, back there,' he said inclining his head, 'it was pretty obvious that you don't know this desert as well as Stony Harte is supposed to. Also,' Voorman went on, 'you're too young to be Harte. As much hell as he has raised in the Territory over the years, why you plain wouldn't have had the time.'

'It was all a frame.'

'But,' Voorman persisted, 'the way they caught you . . . you must know Harte. You must have ridden with him. A part of his gang?'

'Yes,' Cameron said. The lies he had told to stay alive came easier now.

'I thought so. Stony didn't want anyone alive who knew where he had stashed the loot, right? And so he tried to kill you and left his gear and his horse to convince everyone that you were him.'

'That's about it,' Cameron said quietly, and it was very close to the truth if not a perfect fit.

'All that being so,' Voorman said with a smile, 'I guess you've as much reason to want to find Stony Harte as anyone.'

There was no denying that! Voorman nodded, satisfied with his own deductions and he started the weary bay horse on again, Cameron following after.

They had ridden no more than an hour when Voorman reined in again and lifted a joyous pointing finger. 'Look, I told you! I know what I see.'

Cameron's eyes followed the indicated direction and now he could see that in the distance was indeed a collection of buildings, small as dice at this distance, and in several windows lights no brighter than sparks shined.

'I said there was a pueblo ahead,' Voorman said, still enjoying his small triumph. He wiped his perspiring forehead with his sleeve and added, 'Let's get on down there while it's still full dark. If we can avoid dogs we might be able to do ourselves some good.'

Cameron did not like the skulking feeling that come over him as they walked their weary ponies through the night toward the tiny pueblo with its scattering of adobe brick buildings. There were no sounds but once a large dog barked, deep in its throat, far across the town. A voice shouted it to silence and the two escaped prisoners rode on warily.

Voorman whispered to Cameron. 'We'll leave the ponies here, behind that tumbledown shack. It's easier to do this kind of work afoot.'

Cameron nodded and swung down, leading both horses behind an adobe-walled building with a caved-in brush roof. One of the walls had come apart as well and a few bricks were scattered across the yard.

Voorman's eyes were still on him; he could feel their gaze in the night, or believed he could.

Cameron was tempted briefly to make his try then and there, but where could he go but back out onto the desert, and the horses were unfit for further riding? He returned to where Voorman waited and the two burglars slipped off through the night to see what they could accomplish.

SIX

They had discussed what they meant to do once they reached the dark pueblo, but so much depended on chance. The first item of business was to find other clothing. Being seen in their prison rags would be cause for them to be captured and held for a possible reward – if they weren't shot outright by irate townspeople.

Their stealth was remarkable. Moving on their toes among the houses, their long shadows cast by the moon preceding them, they came upon a clothes-line. Cameron kept his eyes on the rear window of the squat house beside it as Voorman collected what he could. They had to find a second line and loot it before they had two ill-fitting white peon outfits. The spare clothes they stashed in a dry rain barrel. There would be some unhappy laundresses in the village come morning.

Next, of course, came fresh horses. These

would be more difficult to come by. Horses are generally watched more closely than laundry. They inched between buildings where the darkness was total. When they had to pass an alley the moonlight was startling in its brilliance. Not knowing the layout of the pueblo, they were at a great disadvantage. Once right in their path a front door opened to a small adobe and a big man in a nightshirt stepped outside to light a cigar and calmly study the moon and low stars. They waited, frozen in position until finally the man carefully stubbed out his cigar butt on the side of the house, scratched himself vigorously and re-entered the adobe.

They moved on swiftly. A black cat, startled at their approach, ran off in silence, swallowed up in seconds by the deep shadows. Voorman put a restraining hand out and gestured for Cameron to use his nose. Perplexed for a moment, Cameron suddenly understood what the Dutchman meant. The smell of old hay and fresh droppings was full in the night air. There was a horse barn or a corral somewhere nearby. Voorman crept forward in a crouch and Cameron Black followed him.

Rounding the corner of the large building to their left they came upon a peaceful-looking scene. A pole corral made of crooked unbarked limbs rested there, and in the corral half-a-dozen horses dozed, their coats sheened by moonlight. Voorman halted and crouched lower, pointing to a tiny adobe structure with a corrugated iron roof to the right. It was just large enough for storing hay and tack.

The Dutchman whispered, 'If there's a stable-man around, he'll be sleeping in the shack.'

Cameron nodded his understanding and they crept forward. The shack's door stood open to the summer night and they saw a bundled figure curled up on some oat sacks in one corner. He had a wide straw sombrero with a red sash tied around the crown placed over his face. Voorman glanced at Cam, his eyes dark and glittering. He made a striking motion with one hand then crept toward the sleeping stablehand's bed. Cameron saw Voorman's hand rise and strike down and saw the figure tense and then go limp.

Voorman tossed the rock he had used aside and said in a low voice, 'Pick two horses out for us and saddle them.'

'What are you going to do?'

'Bind and gag this one. He might come to and we don't want any yelling.'

Cameron's heart was thudding heavily as he crept back toward the pens. Two of the horses were now awake, eyeing him warily. Before Cameron could catch the first pony by its tether and throw the saddle on its back, the Dutchman had returned wearing the sleeping man's sombrero. 'That sun is baking my brains,' Voorman said, as he noticed Cameron's eyes on the hat.

'You didn't spend much time tying him up,' Cameron commented in a low voice. 'Are you sure he won't get loose?'

'He'll be all right,' Voorman said, and then Cameron saw Voorman slip the long awl he had been carrying into the top of his boot. Cameron shuddered a little and got back to his rapid saddling.

Was there a faint gray light emerging from the nightscape to the east? How long was it until dawn? Cameron had lost track of time. He hurried even faster, his fingers feeling thick as he fumbled with the cinches. One of the ponies refused to take the bit and Cameron forced it roughly, caring more for escape than the horse's tender mouth.

'We've got to blow town,' Cameron hissed as they swung aboard. Voorman shook his head.

'We get supplies. Maybe we can break into a store.'

Cameron glanced eastward uneasily as they slowly walked their horses out of the alley. Now he was sure of it: the eastern sky was slowly lightening with false dawn. Inwardly he moaned. Nothing seemed to bother Voorman. The Dutchman's blood was ice cold.

They walked their horses slowly down the main street, passing a central fountain in the tiny plaza. Voorman was still looking for a store to break into. In the gaps between the buildings now, Cameron could see dull flashes of red and of crimson as the sun began to crest the horizon. It seemed as if a giant hand was squeezing his heart in a fierce grip. People, one by one, were emerging from their places of rest. Stretching, buttoning shirts, yawning as they prepared to face a new day. Voorman seemed oblivious to all of it.

Without gesture or word he turned his stolen horse up an alleyway cluttered with rubble and Cameron, glancing at the front of the building saw that Voorman had found his store. They rounded the building with the full glare of brilliant sunrise in their eyes. Voorman swung down without hesitation and approached the rear door of the store. In a moment he had shouldered through.

Cameron swung down to join him, but Voorman met him at the doorway with two canteens.

'Get back to that fountain – you saw it? – fill these and be quick about it.'

Cameron nodded and started that way, keeping now to the backs of the buildings and off the main street. A rooster crowed and was answered by another. A two-year-old child wearing only a shirt stared at Cameron with wide brown eyes as he passed, skirting a tiny corn patch.

Reaching the fountain, Cameron found that he wouldn't be alone for long. Two women both thickly built, one with a basket full of laundry balanced on her head, were approaching leisurely, gossiping the morning away. Cameron let the stolen horse wander away a little from him and strode to the fountain, immersing the canteens. His heart still raced. There would be no mercy for them if they were caught in the pueblo on stolen horses. A yellow dog sniffed at his pant leg and then sat down to bathe indifferently.

Cameron hefted the canteens and corked them just as the women arrived, placing the laundry basket on the ground. He had turned his back to them and started away when the cry went up. His heart froze, he began to stride rapidly toward his horse, fear propelling him. But it wasn't him that the cry had gone up against.

Glancing up the street he could see three or four men, at least one of them with a machete, following a woman in a black skirt and red, collarless blouse toward the back of the store Voorman had entered. Her words were shrill but indistinct. She hoisted her skirt with one hand and pointed with the other. He made out the words *sombrero . . . rojo*, and knew the game was up. The woman had spotted Voorman and seen the sombrero with the distinctive red scarf, perhaps a woman's favor, used for a hat band.

Other men joined the pursuit. At the uproar, every doorway and window filled with curious brown faces. Cameron dropped the canteens out of sight and abandoned the horse. He dared not try to ride it out of town now. It, too, was probably a known inhabitant of the pueblo. He started slowly toward the store, deciding that to hurry in the opposite direction would only draw attention to him. He joined the crowd, hanging on the fringe of it, just another curious villager. Men stood on a wooden boardwalk in front of the cantina, watching speculatively. These were not Mexicans, but Americanos. Tall men wearing belted guns and high Texas boots.

And among them was a man with a wildly deformed nose, cruel eyes and misshapen jaw. *Willie Durant!* This member of Stony Harte's gang had a face that could not be mistaken. There he stood, thumbs hooked into his belt, a crooked, clumsily rolled cigarette dangling from his battered lips. Cameron turned his face and walked on more quickly. He could hear the voices of the men standing in front of the saloon.

'What's up, Willie?' someone asked. 'I don't understand that lingo.'

'Somebody killed the old lady's husband over

to the stables. She found him when she brought breakfast to him. Says she saw some stranger by the store wearing her man's hat.'

'Well, that just wasn't real smart of him, was it?' the other man laughed.

'They'll chop him to bits for sure,' Willie answered. 'I seen 'em work with those machetes before.'

The conversation continued but Cameron could make out no more of it. He went on, jostled now and then by someone rushing to the scene. He slowed to a walk, looked for escape and shunted into a narrow alley where he halted. Doubled over he braced himself with one hand against the adobe wall, trying to catch his breath and quiet his heartbeat.

They had caught Voorman and justice would be swift. Cameron was out of luck. Alone again in a strange land. Maybe, he thought, the other nags were where they had left them – behind the tumbledown shack on the outskirts of the pueblo. What use were they? Those old plugs had broken down long back and he still faced travel on the desert without food or water.

He was trapped and beaten for sure. His every instinct was simply to flee and let Fate take its course. Let him die on the desert. That seemed to be what was intended for him one way or the other. But slowly as his breathing stilled and his heart rate dropped to something near normal, he began to feel a different sort of emotion wash over him in surging waves. Hatred. A cold hatred. He had been doomed by one man: the man who had pretended to be his friend.

Stony Harte.

If Willie was here, in this tiny pueblo, could Stony be far away?

He could still hear the crowd's uproar and he closed his eyes tightly for a moment, not wanting to think what those men with the machetes were doing to the Dutchman. Cameron had come to despise Voorman and knew him for a murderer, but he wouldn't wish that on any man.

His thoughts clearing, his breath regained, he began to think of survival. Two horses missing from the stable. One saddled, apparently owner-less, pony near the plaza's fountain. It wouldn't take the villagers long to realize that there was another intruder among them and that he was probably afoot. Cameron started toward the shanty where they had left their own weary mounts. The roan couldn't be pushed far or fast, but it surely had five more miles in it. Enough to get him clear of the pueblo precinct.

The sun was rising higher, growing white and hot across the vast desert as Cameron hurried on. He rounded the broken-down hovel with his breath coming in panting gasps – like those of the horned toad he had seen.

The horses were gone.

Cursing, Cameron pounded the side of his fist against the crumbling adobe wall of the outbuilding.

All right, then! What were his options? To attempt to mingle among the pueblo's inhabitants, a stranger in a land where strangers were few, seemed futile. He would be pointed out in moments. Except . . . there was the cantina where white cowboys and travelers hung out. There he would not have to hide his face for its color. Of course, there was *Willie* to be considered, but Cameron didn't think the gunman would risk shooting him down in this small town where judgement on him, too, would be sure and swift. Perhaps so, but there were few other courses of action that he could think of.

Cameron began slinking down the morning alley again, assuming the cantina would have some sort of back or side door for deliveries and carrying out its refuse. He stayed off the main street where the villagers still clogged every foot of open space cursing or passing information or yelling out words he could not understand.

Finding the back door to the cantina he hesitated. There were three steps to mount and then a sun-bleached wooden door. There was no telling what lay beyond the door, and Cameron had become in turns a convict, an escaped felon and presumed accomplice in two murders! Steeling himself, he stepped forward, mounted the steps and, holding his breath, reached for the latch, hoping it was not locked from the interior. He could hear voices not far away, perhaps men searching for the second American. He stretched out a hand to open the door, but it was swung open abruptly before his hand reached the latch.

'Come in, quickly,' the young Spanish girl said, and Cameron, hypnotized by the urgency in the bright-eyed girl's voice, did as he was commanded.

He found himself inside a dark room smelling of stale beer and sawdust, crates and barrels stacked high against two walls. 'Follow me,' the girl said. She was around five feet four inches tall, wore a white skirt and blouse of the Spanish style. Her raven hair was glossy and pinned up in some method Cameron was unfamiliar with. For jewelry she wore silver hoop ear-rings and one tiny silver ring with entwined strands. Her eyes were large and frank, her mouth was not wide, but her full underlip made it seem so.

'Hurry up; what are you looking at?' she demanded, although she must have known. 'There is no time to waste. I have heard all about it. They will cut you to ribbons if we don't hide you now.'

He followed blindly, trusting the girl because there was no other choice. And, he admitted, he believed in her dark eyes.

Opening a door they stepped into a narrow hallway. Now Cameron could hear music – two guitars – from a room beyond playing some sort of gypsy melody with an intriguing refrain. He didn't have time to dwell on the tune or its composition. They quickly reached a narrow internal stairway. The Spanish girl paused, placed a finger of silence to her lips, lifted her white skirt a few inches and crept up it, glancing back once across her shoulder to make sure Cameron was following.

The room she led him to was neat, clean, organized. There was a woman's touch to every corner of it. Bright shawls, woven bedspread, splashily colored hangings. She toed a high-backed wooden chair out and gestured for him to seat himself as she returned to the door, looked up and down the corridor, closed the door and returned to sit opposite him in a matching dark-wood chair.

'They won't find you here unless you act stupid.'

'I won't,' Cameron answered, still puzzled by her sudden appearance and concern over him.

Silence clung to the room for a long while as the white curtains covering the partially opened window of the room billowed in the light breeze. Far away, it seemed, men still shouted like hunting pack animals.

'Why are you doing this?' he asked, when he couldn't contain the question any longer.

'How could I not?' she replied simply, smoothing her skirt. A breath of warm air from outside shifted a slender tendril of dark hair across her forehead. She brushed it away as if it were an annoying insect.

'You don't know who I am,' Cameron said, and to his astonishment the girl broke out in laughter – sweet, innocent laughter.

'Of course I do, you dope!' she answered, using the last word as if it were new to her, an affectation.

'But you can't!'

'But I can, Cameron Black,' the girl replied quietly, her gaze fixed on him. 'I do know who you are.'

'But how. . . ?'

'Your face,' she said, with a shrug, the palms of her hands turned up. 'I knew the moment I saw you. No one could look so much like Stony Harte if it wasn't you.'

'Look . . . I'm sorry I don't know your name.'

'Carmalita.'

'Carmalita,' Cameron said, trying the sound of it, 'you seem to be a pretty straightforward woman, but you're running rings around my mind. I can't quite catch up, if you know what I mean. How could you know me? How in the world could you know anything about Stony Harte?'

'It is simple. Where shall I start to explain?' She touched the tip of her finger to her cheek, making a mock-dimple. 'Have you not met a woman called Emily? A stout woman? When you were with Stony Harte?' Cameron nodded mutely. Yes, he remembered the woman in the cabin at Stony's hideout.

'Emily is my sister . . . well, she is my half-sister, really. We had different fathers. Emily,' she said, after a small pause, 'fell in with this Stony Harte, this *cabron*. Do you know that term?' she asked.

'No.'

'No matter, it is not a polite term in any language, but that is what he is.' Carmalita's Spanish accent came and went like a voice bent by the wind. It was mystifying, Cameron thought, and quite charming.

'You haven't told me yet how you could know about me,' he said.

'No.' She rose, elegantly and smoothly and walked to the window to close it. 'The breeze that cools and enlivens the morning turns to a devil wind by noon. It will blow hot dust in and . . . that's not what you wanted to hear.' She seated herself again, clasped hands between her knees. 'Emily is my half-sister, she is older than me, and she is quite wild. She has been since her father died. She runs with bad men. It is so. She tells me that they have more money to spend than any peon could hope to see, and they live exciting lives. I have heard all of her tales.

'A year or so ago she met this man, this Stony Harte, and rode away with his gang. I do not ask her what chores she performs, if you understand me. Emily thinks that Stony Harte loves her, that she would die for him. I don't know where she gets such romantic nonsense. Do you know the term "camp-follower"?'

'Yes.'

'That is what my sister is, though for an outlaw band. She fantasizes about Harte, but I think he is just a . . . bad man,' she said, avoiding the earlier crude term she had used. 'Emily has told me about all of Stony Harte's great exploits and how clever he is. She told me that Stony had the law on his trail and so he killed a man who looked enough like him to make the law think he was Stony Harte, that Stony Harte was dead. Let me see,' Carmalita said, rising again. The delicate touch of her fingers was pleasant as she examined Cameron's skull, finding the furrowed, roughly stitched scar. She drew her breath in faintly. 'I knew it was so. It had to be you. Except they did not kill you dead enough.'

Cameron laughed; the girl frowned.

'So now what do you wish to do?' Carmalita asked. 'Find Stony Harte and kill him?'

'Yes,' Cameron Black heard himself say. He had not phrased it that way even to himself, but it was true, wasn't it?

'I will help you,' Carmalita said, and now there was no humor in her dark eyes. None at all.

SEVEN

Cameron sat silently watching the girl's eager eyes, the quirky half-smile on her anxious mouth, wondering if what he had just said was true. In a way it was – Stony Harte deserved death, but he did not really want it to be at his own hands. He doubted if he was capable of such an act. He tried to explain his feelings to Carmalita.

'I hate the man, but I could not kill him. I am not built that way, Carmalita. All I wanted was to make my way to Tombstone. I had hopes of finding a job there. I am peace-loving and, I suppose, too soft for the wild country.'

'Gentle,' she suggested. Cameron shrugged.

'Choose whatever term you care to,' he replied. He rubbed at his forehead, sunburned and aching. 'My only chance of survival – I have thought long about this – is to take Stony Harte to the authorities. And he would be a dangerous man to try to capture. This I know.' Carmalita started to interrupt, but Cam held up his hand and went on. 'The other chance would be to restore the stolen gold to the stage line. There is a man named Morton who has his office in Tucson, an agent for Wells Fargo. He seemed to be a fair-minded man. If I could find the gold and deliver it to him, I might be exonerated.'

'Can it be done?' Carmalita wondered.

'I have no idea. It is Stony Harte we're dealing with,' Cameron answered, realizing that he had used a plural. 'This man can shoot the head off a rattlesnake without aiming. I know, I've seen him in action.'

'So Emily has told me,' the girl said, biting at her lower lip. 'It is good to know that everything she tells me is not a lie.'

'I don't see—'

'Because my sister tells me many things, Cameron Black – more, I'm sure than the outlaws would like, if they knew about it. Let us discuss this matter, carefully discuss it.'

'I don't get it,' Cameron said, rising to walk to the window. He parted the curtains and looked out at the plaza which seemed to have returned to relative calm.

'Get?'

'Understand,' he explained to the Spanish

106

girl. 'You seem to be offering to help me, but I don't even know you, Carmalita! How can I be sure—?'

'That I am not in love with Stony Harte, working to see that you are jailed, wanting any reward that might be offered for you, trying to keep you prisoner?'

'Well. . . .' he said hesitantly, but his words were banished by her wild laughter – not hysterical or mocking, but simply exuberantly merry.

She wiped tears of laughter from her huge brown eyes with the hem of her white skirt, folded her arms beneath her breasts and told him, 'None of that is so. I despise Stony Harte for what he has done to my sister, what she has become. If I wanted you killed I would not have opened the door for you. If I wanted a reward, I would not be alone with you in a room you are free to leave at any time. I could not stop you; I'm sure you are much stronger than I am. No, Cameron Black, I simply want to escape from Las Colinas – that is the name of this pueblo if you did not know, and free my sister of this strange infatuation she has with these outlaws.' She shrugged and continued, 'I know there have been many women who attach themselves to such men, perhaps seeing them as exciting rebels like Robin Hood. I am young, but I know this is not so. These people are nothing but animals. I can see how they treat Emily and it is ruining her as a woman.'

'All right,' Cameron said, taking her at her word. He turned to face the young Spanish woman 'What is your idea of how to proceed?'

'I can see your eyes,' Carmalita responded, rising to face him. 'What you wish most is to be safe. That means we have to find a way to smuggle you out of the pueblo. The second thing I see in your eyes, Cameron Black, is that you wish to take revenge on Stony Harte, but are not sure how to go about it.'

'True,' he admitted.

'My priorities are different, but our aims are the same. I want firstly to remove Emily from the hands of the bandits. Secondly only, I wish to take some small measure of revenge on Stony Harte. He has not injured me so grievously as you, yet still I hate him.'

'Has he ever tried. . . ?' Cameron asked weakly.

'To have me follow in Emily's footsteps. Of course!' she laughed, but there was no humor in her laughter.

Cameron rubbed his forehead with the heel of his hand. 'Maybe I should just try again to get to Tombstone on my own, leave all of this behind me. I don't think I'm a coward, Carmalita, but I don't think I'm man enough to go up against Stony and his gang. They have a special sort of murderous skill that I do not possess.'

'You must do what you want,' the girl said sharply and she turned her back to him. She still clutched herself, her back showing beneath her white blouse fit tightly across her shoulders. She was silent then. Cameron lifted a hand meaninglessly. Without turning to face him, Carmalita asked, 'Would it help if I begged for your help? I am a woman alone; I can do nothing.'

Then Cameron did feel like a coward. His heart sank as he studied her. It wasn't his pride in his manhood nor the beauty of the slender lines of her body that swayed him: it was her foundationless trust in him, a childlike hope that he might assist her that shamed him. His hand rose again and this time he stepped nearer and placed it on her shoulder.

'All right, then,' he said without the reluctance he was feeling. 'You've been thinking this through longer than I have. Where are they and how do we go about it?'

They sat at the small table where Carmalita had placed two dainty cups filled with strong coffee. The sun slanted through the window, etching rectangles on the floor. Once, outside, there was a huge uproar and Carmalita explained, 'They are dragging the murderer's body through the town,' and then the silence returned. Cameron hadn't liked the Dutchman at the end when he had reverted to his true colors, but he hated to think of any man's life ending as Voorman's had.

'Are there still just the three of them?' Cameron asked, referring to Stony Harte's gang. 'Stony, Willie and the man called Slyke?'

'That is all,' Carmalita answered, as the sun through the pale curtains lit the dark gloss of her hair with its brilliance.

'Of course. If they brought anyone else in at this point they'd have to split the gold another way.'

'That is so,' Carmalita agreed. 'And if there were ten men instead of three, it would draw attention. A band of men that size would alert people that trouble might be arriving. Cameron,' the girl said, revolving her cup on its saucer but never sipping the coffee, 'two of the men, Willie and Slyke – I did not know that was his name – the one with a head like an egg, no hair even on his face – are staying in rooms at the cantina.'

'And Stony Harte?' Cameron Black asked, and astonishingly the girl blushed and turned her eyes down in shame.

'They are at my mother's house. Las Colinas is my home, as you know. And it is my sister's.

My mother is very old and she is nearly blind, half deaf, quite infirm. It is so sad that Emily has told my mother that Stony is her Americano husband. My mother feels a little sad because my sister has married a *gringo*; if she knew the truth of what Stony is, I believe it would be her death.'

'I understand.'

'When Emily and her "husband" come home from a business trip – buying horses is what they say, selling them in Mexico – they bring presents for Mama and Emily hugs her and Mama is so happy, glad that her daughter has everything she needs.' Carmalita hesitated. 'She does not know that Stony Harte is a robber, a gunman. She does not see the way he treats Emily. How he beats her and curses her and calls her names.'

'Emily takes it?'

'She takes it, covers her bruises and crawls back like a beaten bitch.'

'I understand now, a little more, why you hate Stony,' Cameron replied. 'And all the time, does he—?'

'Yes, of course!' Carmalita answered. 'All the time he takes every chance to try to grab me, threaten me, tell me how beautiful I am, how much gold he would give me.' Her face finally lifted and although she had not been crying,

111

Cameron could see the hidden tears in her eyes. His resolve was growing stronger. He himself had been shot, left for dead, imprisoned, but somehow that had already begun to fade from memory. He had survived.

But the heartbreak in Carmalita's voice was much more touching than his own sorrows. He did not believe for a moment that he was strong enough to best a hardened killer like Stony Harte, but he had resolved that he was strong enough to *try*.

'It's better to go after the two in the cantina first,' Cameron said, after a long period of thought. 'Do they drink enough to muddle their thinking?' He recalled the 'white lightning' the gang members had had at the hideout cabin. Raw spirits, as close to pure alcohol as could be distilled.

Carmalita told him, 'They get drunk, flirt with the girls, try to start fights and sometimes fall down on the cantina floor. The owner does not care – they spend money very freely. Always in gold.'

'I wonder what Stony thinks of that?' Cameron mused.

'I can tell you. Listening at their bedroom door, I have heard Stony tell Emily that he was going to ditch the two of them. I don't understand that word in that sense, but if it means what

I think it does, Slyke and Willie will never get their share of the remaining gold. He gives them just enough to stay drunk on.'

'That makes sense from Harte's point of view. And, by the way, the word means to leave someone on the side of the road, in a ditch.'

'That is what I thought,' Carmalita said, with a seriousness that almost made Cameron burst out laughing. She again bit at her underlip as she pondered the real gravity of Harte's deviousness. A sincere, strong and yet childlike woman she was a refreshingly bright strain of some new blossom in Cameron's eyes, and in his heart. He chased his boyish thoughts away. Who was he, after all, even to hope for such a woman to stand with him? He, himself, was an escaped convict, a penniless desert coyote going nowhere – unless Tombstone with the vague and menial prospect of gaining a job as a muleteer could be called *somewhere.*

'We'll eliminate those two first,' Cameron said.

'How?' Carmalita asked.

'I don't know. But Stony alone is still only one man. We'll take care of Willie and Slyke some way.'

'Murder!'

'Carmalita,' Cameron Black said, extending his hand across the small table, 'I cannot murder. Thank God I am incapable of that act.'

113

She took his hand and her grip was warm, gentle and yet still strong. She was that sort of woman. 'But we will find a way. Let's think a little more about it.'

One thing still bothered him deeply. 'Emily. She won't want to leave Stony. What are we to do, kidnap her? You know you can't convince her in minutes – you must have tried that.'

'If it must be done,' Carmalita said, with the determination of a child-woman, 'I will kidnap her! I will not let my sister be turned into a whipped dog.'

And that was all there was to that. At least in the quite-resolute Carmalita's mind. Before he told her what he had in mind for the outlaws, Cameron looked deeply into her Spanish eyes and said frankly, 'Carmalita, you must understand one thing: I am not Robin Hood or Jesse James either.'

Their hands still touched and she squeezed his slightly. 'I know that . . . this makes you better, you see, Cameron Black. You know you are not invincible and yet you are willing to try despite your doubts and fears. For me. This makes you better than they were. You, Cameron Black, are a *man*.'

Their plan was risky, but both knew they could not hope to snatch Emily from Stony Harte's grip if all the while they had to watch their backs for the two other Harte gunmen who might appear at any time. The decision they came to was not one Cameron Black liked, but he admitted it was the likeliest ploy toward success.

It all centered on Carmalita and her desirability. Slyke and Willie both knew her, of course, if by sight alone, and once they were in their cups, they were bound to have their lower instincts aroused if it seemed Carmalita was a woman of promise. That was the part of the plan Cameron did not like. In fact, it revulsed him, but if there were any way to lure one of the gunmen away from the cantina crowd and keep him off his guard, this was it. It was difficult to imagine any man spurning Carmalita's advances, and one in a drunken state would give no thought to the possible hazards beyond his own desires.

'I don't like it,' Cameron said one more time.

'*I* do not like it,' Carmalita said simply. 'Is there another way?'

'Not that I can think of,' he answered unhappily.

'Then, we look to the goal and not to the method.'

There was no way to plan against all contingencies. There were too many variables. What they intended to do was remove Slyke and Willie Durant from the scene long enough so they could be sure of facing Stony Harte alone. Not that he alone was not enough of a challenge, but the odds were better nonetheless. All of it was to be done long after darkness fell, the closer to midnight the better. By then, as was their custom, Stony's henchmen should be well in their cups and Stony himself asleep in Emily's bed. Carmalita's mother would also be asleep at that time – Cameron meant to cause her no more distress than necessary.

The day slogged past in hot white lethargy. The flies buzzed around the room. Children played in the streets, pursued by happy dogs. Cameron dozed stiffly in the wooden chair, his folded arms growing cramped. Each time he opened his eyes, however, there was Carmalita, awake and alert, looking through the curtains or glancing expectantly at the door to her room. He watched once as, weary with concern and grief over her sister, she leaned her fist against the wall and placed her forehead against it. Her shoulders trembled slightly with a sob, but she shook herself out of the mood and began straightening the already tidy room with nervous efficiency. She was a strong woman, and a bold one, this Spanish girl, and Cameron felt guilty about the pangs of doubt he held. Doubts of his own ability to rescue the situation. She had so much confidence in him, and yet he was forced

116

to consider if he was up to the task.

The slanting sunbeams took on a more horizontal angle and then were devoured by purple dusk. Cameron still pretended to sleep although he needed to be up and moving. The waiting was enervating. There was no clock in the room, but he knew it was still too soon to make their try. He rose stiffly and walked to the window, staring out at the pueblo. Lamps and candles went off at intervals and there was the singing of the cicadas, the chirping of the crickets announcing the night's entry.

'Shall we go?' he asked Carmalita, who had placed a dark shawl across her shoulders and she nodded.

'I can't endure waiting any longer.' She glided rather than walked to him and placed a heavy object in his hand. 'I don't know if this is in fine order, but I thought it was a good thing for you to have. It was my father's.'

It was an ancient Walker Colt, heavy and old-fashioned, the model they used to call a 'horse pistol' because it was carried on the pommel of a saddle, being too heavy for a man's holstered leg. It had been kept in good repair, and recently oiled, it seemed. 'It will do what it was designed to do,' Cameron said, examining the .44 revolver.

He thrust it behind his belt and drew a deep

breath. 'I like none of this, Carmalita,' he said, looking down into her hopeful eyes.

'Nor do I, Cameron Black, but we will do what must be done.'

They went out into the boisterous corridor of the cantina.

Below, men drank, smoked, shouted, gambled and cursed. A woman's shrill laugh rang out above the rumble of the male din.

With gestures, Carmalita urged Cameron Black into the storeroom at the foot of the stairs where all was silent and dim. Poking around as she moved away, he found a spool of waxed twine on a workbench. It was strong enough to do their work if Carmalita's plan did not fail. Hoisting himself onto a crate Cameron Black decided that it could not fail. What man would not accompany her wherever she asked him to? Cam didn't like to think what nasty, spidery thoughts could crawl through the mind of the gunman. He sat, alert with nervousness, and waited.

The cantina was alive with the whirl of dancers and the roaring laughter of the drinking men. Carmalita was not troubled by it. She had taken the upstairs room a long time ago when it became obvious that Emily would return frequently to her home with Stony Harte. She hated that man and needed to stay away from her mother's house. Mostly the men who came to the cantina just drank too much and acted like silly boys. She paid them no mind, and she was afforded courtesy.

But on this night her slashing eyes were alert to every gesture and face. Both of Harte's accomplices were there, though widely separated. The bald man, Slyke, stood at the bar, foot on the brass rail, hat tilted back. His partner, Willie, the one with the badly mangled nose sat in the far corner, holding a girl she knew only as Alicia on his lap. Now and then Alicia would try to rise and escape, but Willie kept her there by force, laughing at each attempt.

Which one? It did not matter, Carmalita decided. She had been steeling herself for this moment all day long. Now, like an actress confident in her role, she walked to the long, scarred bar and positioned herself beside Slyke who looked up at her with pleased surprise.

'Hello, doll!' Slyke said, adjusting his hat over his bald head. 'I seen you around here, haven't I?'

'I work here,' Carmalita answered. 'I live here.'

'Is that so?' Slyke said, drinking a shot of whiskey. His very words, blatant in their implicit meaning caused Carmalita's body to tense; her stomach seemed to shrink and grow hard. There was too much at stake to show any fear or doubts.

119

She placed a falsely bright smile on her mouth.

'That is so,' she answered, and she could feel Slyke's eyes disrobing her.

'Well, well,' the gunman said. 'Nice we could talk. Would you like something to drink?' He leaned nearer and Carmalita could smell his reek. His entire body smelled something like a badly rotted tooth. She tried her smile again; it was almost painful to do so as the badman continued to watch her with glazed yellowish eyes. But Slyke saw only what he wanted to see.

'I do not like what they serve,' Carmalita told him. 'I only drink Madeira.'

'Is that so? Well, where can we get some of that, doll? I'll buy you some!' he said, growing expansive, and too obviously drawing a twenty-dollar gold piece from the pocket of his jeans. Carmalita felt herself seeming to shrink again. How could any of these women live like this and have any self-respect! How could Emily. . . ?

'I have a good bottle of wine in my room. Upstairs,' she said, gesturing with her head. 'I don't know if you would like Madeira. . . .'

'Doll,' Slyke said, tugging the brim of his hat even lower with a wink, 'I like anything you like.'

Glancing around the room, a movement Slyke probably took for caution but which Carmalita actually used to turn her eyes away from the slug of a man, she answered as she had practiced, 'Well, just for one drink, it might be allowed, sir.'

Slyke's grin threatened to separate his face into different spheres as he tossed down the last of his whiskey and motioned with his hand.

'Let's go. Later we can decide what's allowed.'

And Carmalita was still smiling brightly as she swirled her skirt once and led the gunhand toward the staircase. Her only thought was:

Let this work!

EIGHT

'There's nothing to it,' Cameron Black was thinking as he watched the cantina from the storeroom, the door open only an inch or so. Grab the
man from behind, club him down. He won't
know what hit him.

It didn't go so simply.

The first sounds he heard were Carmalita's
heels clicking against the wooden floor. Then
came the shuffling of boot leather. He caught a
glimpse of the man's face in the poor light. It was
Slyke. She had chosen Slyke first. Cameron
slipped the horse pistol from behind his belt and
hefted the heavy, ancient Walker.

Cameron's idea was a simple one, to crack
Slyke's skull with the revolver, drag him into the
storeroom and bind him. Like many other things
that seem simple in their conception, this proved
to be anything but in its execution.

Just as Slyke stepped past the door of

Cameron's hiding place, Black stepped out, trying to bash the outlaw on the head with the barrel of the old Colt. Slyke saw the movement and instinctively ducked and turned away. The pistol barrel glanced off Slyke's head, doing little damage. Slyke hollered out furiously and they could only hope that the racket in the cantina muffled his voice enough so that no one could hear and rush to his aid.

Cameron tried again to club down Slyke, but the bald-headed man's hands found his throat and clamped down like two vises. Cameron failed to break the hold of the frenzied outlaw. He lifted one foot and slammed the heel of his boot into Slyke's leg, behind the knee joint. Slyke grunted, lost his balance and fell over on top of Cameron in the rank little room. The pistol went clattering free and lost itself in the shadows.

Instead of covering her mouth in horror or shrinking away, Carmalita hurled herself onto Slyke's back and began pummeling his head and back with her small fists. Slyke tried to brush her away with one hand, but to do so he had to give up his grip on Cameron's throat. In a blind panic, Cameron drove his right fist into Slyke's face, catching him just below the ear. It may have stunned him slightly, but the outlaw gave no sign of it.

'His gun!' Cameron shouted, and Carmalita

dove on Slyke's back again, pawing at his holstered Colt Army. Slyke clamped her hand with his as she tried to draw the weapon from its holster and that freed Cameron's other hand. He drove his left fist into Slyke's eye twice as Slyke cursed at him, sprayed spittle and writhed like a captured wildcat. Cameron tried to drive his knee up into Slyke's body, but the bald man had him pinned to the floor.

Carmalita had the outlaw's gun now and she began to use the butt of it as a weapon. All of her blows were delivered glancingly as Slyke rolled from side to side with wild anger. To defend himself from the onslaught Slyke had to change his position and Cameron was able to wriggle free from his weight, striking Slyke twice more, once on the cheek, splitting it to the bone, once on the throat which caused Slyke to roar a strangled curse.

Inches away, Cameron now saw the ancient Walker revolver and he struggled toward it as Carmalita, her eyes wide, her hair in wild disarray, beat on Slyke. Cameron's fingers stretched to the Walker and he brought it around fiercely. The blow landed just as Carmalita's last strike with Slyke's own gun cracked off the outlaw's skull.

It was enough. The wildly resisting Slyke went limp, his body across Cameron's legs, his hand still resting on Black's throat. More quickly than he would have thought possible, Cameron scooted away from Slyke's weight and sat panting on the floor, holding his own head.

He was breathing raggedly. There was blood leaking from his nose. Carmalita had begun to tremble.

'I don't think we are so very good at this yet,' she said shakily. 'Do we tie him up now?'

'We tie him quickly, efficiently, thoroughly,' Cameron said, rising to his feet. He looked down at the motionless Slyke. 'He didn't look that strong, did he?'

'I don't like fighting after this,' Carmalita said. Her voice had become more inflected, more Spanish. She was obviously shaken.

'I don't either,' Cameron said, grabbing the spool of twine they would use to tie Slyke. 'Unfortunately, we've only begun.'

Willie, thankfully, was less trouble. The badman was nearly blind drunk when Carmalita, after pinning her hair up, again returned to the cantina to lure the redhead with his savaged face after her toward the stairs. Her walk was careless and inviting, but Cameron could see the tension behind it. Willie bounced off the walls of the narrow corridor as he followed. It may have been that his drunkenness was what made it easier, but it took no time at all to strike him down.

Cameron had always thought of himself as a

merciful man, but there was no mercy in him just then. Perhaps it was fear that impelled him – he knew that he didn't want to go through another fight like the one he had just had with Slyke. When Willie passed half a step beyond the door to the storeroom, Cameron slipped behind him and drove the muzzle of the Walker Colt behind the outlaw's ear with every ounce of strength he possessed. Willie slumped soundlessly to the floor and with a glance toward the cantina, Carmalita helped Cam drag the gunman into the room. Both outlaws were left tied, gagged, unconscious, behind the beer barrels scattered around the room.

When they had finished, Cameron stepped back, aching from every joint, feeling his bruises now. Perspiration streamed into his eyes and down his chest. Carmalita stood silently, seeming stunned by what they had accomplished. Then with a toss of her head, she said brightly, 'Good. We have done that. Now these men cannot interfere.

'It is time we get to our real work.'

The real work. Yes, rescuing Emily who probably did not wish to be rescued from the grasp of Stony Harte, the gunman who could pick out a snake's eye with a careless shot from his pistol. Cameron had fully committed himself to the project, but whether it was cowardice or simple wisdom, he wished he could just ride out, flee onto the open desert and take no part in trying to best Stony Harte. In the near darkness of the storeroom, Carmalita's huge Spanish eyes still studied his with misplaced confidence and hope, and he found himself saying simply, 'We'd better have our try now, while it's still full dark.'

The ranchita which was both Emily and Carmalita's childhood home was dark against the darker earth. A cluster of live oaks stood huddled together on one side, a lonely sycamore stood before the small, boxlike house. To one side there was a pair of small outbuildings for farm implements and tack, Cameron guessed. At their slow approach an owl dipped from the sycamore and glided silently away, casting star shadows. The air was warm and dusty, yet above that Cameron could smell water. There must have been a small creek somewhere nearby. Otherwise there was no reason for the ranchita to have been built amidst all of this desolation.

They halted cautiously and Cameron drew Carmalita to the night shade of the dusty oak trees, whispering to her.

'Where will they be?' he asked.

Crouching, she used a twig to draw the floor-plan of the small house. 'One comes in the front door and that is the living-room. The kitchen is just to the left, the largest room in the house. There are only two other rooms beyond. The one on the left is my mother's, the one across the hall is where Stony Harte and Emily will be sleeping.'

'If they are asleep,' Cameron said uncertainly. 'Have you any idea. . . ?'

'About the gold?' Carmalita said, rising to dust off her hands. Her expression was one of concern. Could it be possible that the *gold* was the only reason this man was helping her?

'Don't look at me like that,' he told her. 'You know that I need to return the gold to buy my freedom. Otherwise, we . . . otherwise *I* will be a wanted man the rest of my life, never knowing who is pursuing me.'

'I didn't mean to . . .' she said hesitantly, remembering the words he had started to speak.

'It's all right.' Cameron rubbed his hand across his dark hair. 'I cannot live a hunted man, Carmalita. So, yes, the gold is important to me.'

'I have not seen it. I believe it must be hidden in their room, however, because Stony does not go out without locking the door.'

'All right,' Cameron said grimly as he studied the small adobe house. 'I'll just ask Stony about it. And he *will* tell me, or. . . .'

Or what? He could not murder Stony Harte; even if he could bring himself to do such a thing, a dead Stony Harte could tell him nothing. 'I'll find it,' he swore under his breath, and now he took two slow breaths and nodded. 'Let's do what we came here to do. There is no dog?'

'Not for years,' Cannalita answered, as they began to move toward the house, weaving through the scrawny oaks. Cameron decided to circle the house slowly and unsurprisingly they found a pinto pony, saddled and ready, ground-hitched beneath an open window.

'The man knows his craft,' Cameron Black murmured. Carmalita did not quite hear him or understand him.

They crouched together in the night. The moon was only a dull glaze through the trees. 'What do you think?' Carmalita whispered.

'Knock on the front door,' Cameron told her.

'What? Is that smart?'

'I don't know. You're going in alone,' he said.

'You. . . ?'

Cameron lifted his chin toward the open window which Stony meant to use for any hasty escape. 'I'm going in this way. His attention will be on the front of the house. There's no reason to suspect you. You've just come to see your mother, to come home – use any reason you can think up. Men were annoying you at the cantina; anything, just get Stony's attention on you.'

Carmalita nodded uncertain understanding. Her hand rested briefly on his forearm. 'This is so very dangerous, Cameron Black.'

'Yes,' he replied. 'Yes, it is.' Then he breathed in deeply again, rose and pulled the old revolver from his belt, checking its loads by the scant moonlight. 'Let's do it now, Carmalita, before I lose my nerve.'

She rose beside him, hesitated, kissed his cheek with lips as light as a butterfly, and hurried away, holding up her skirts with both hands. Cameron Black waited, knowing the doors of Hades were about to swing open.

He waited, his back pressed against the wall of the house. The pinto pony, long-legged and deep in the chest as one would expect a man like Harte to ride, stared at him incuriously, working at a few yellow blades of buffalo grass it had pulled up in a clump.

Cameron heard the rapping at the front door, heard a muttered, urgent curse, heard bare feet walk toward the door, a man's steps. He could envision Stony, dressed for bed or naked, carrying a cocked revolver at his side, wary of any night visitors. Using both hands to muffle the lock-click of the hammer, Cameron slowly cocked the big Walker horse pistol.

He waited. Not *yet*. Not yet! – he didn't dare lift his eyes over the window sill until the inner door was opened and a lantern was lighted, the wick turned low. He heard Emily's voice.

'What is it, Stony?'

'How the hell should I know?' he growled. 'Get to the door; see who it is.'

Now Cameron did dare to peek into the room, his heart surging in his ribcage. He saw Emily slip from the bed and throw a wrapper over her. By the door, Stony Harte, wearing only a pair of black jeans stood, his gun held beside his ear as he peered out into the hallway. Beyond, somewhere, a muffled voice weakly repeated '*Que es? Que es?*' so they had awakened the girls' mother as well.

Nothing could be done about that. Cameron waited as Emily slipped past Harte and went to the front door to answer Carmalita's frantic knocking, then, taking advantage of what he hoped was a moment of confusion he hoisted himself up and over the sill into Stony's room. The small sounds he made as his feet struck the floor were enough to alert the experienced criminal. Stony Harte whirled, his face a mask of angry resentment, lip pulled up tightly at one corner. But even Stony's reflexes were not sharp enough for him to turn, fire blindly and pick off a rolling man.

Cameron came to his feet, aimed his revolver and then changed his mind in an instant too quick to be measured. He lunged forward, driving his shoulder into Stony's body, slamming him against the wall as a commotion began beyond the door. There was time for an astonished Stony Harte to shout, 'You!' and then his revolver was fired again, but Cameron's forearm had been rising in anticipation of the shot and Stony's aim was jolted upward, the bullet slamming into the plaster ceiling as the room reverberated with the savage echo of the .44-40.

Cameron drew upon a strength he did not know he had and wrenched the gun away from Stony's hand as his own right hand drove down like a pile driver against Harte's face. Amazingly, the outlaw was knocked cold, his eyes rolling back as he became oblivious to the world.

Beyond the door Emily screamed like a banshee and, yanking the door open scant inches with Stony's weight against it, Cameron saw Carmalita grabbing at her bigger sister's clothing, trying to hold her back. Both women yelled high-pitched Spanish words and Cameron saw a tiny woman, her hair streaked with white, back away, clutching her nightdress to her narrow bosom in confused fear.

Cameron banged the door shut, turned the key and bound Stony with his own belt and a bandanna Stony had stuffed into his hip pocket. Emily drove her shoulder against the door again and Cameron heard the two of them fall in a heap to the floor of the hallway. The old woman prayed pathetically, understanding none of this.

There was the sharp rap of knuckles on the door and Cameron opened it a hair. Carmalita, breathing roughly, told him, 'I've got her down. I hated . . . Cameron, there is a man riding up.'

'Who?'

'I only caught a glimpse as he went past the window. I think it is Slyke! That bald head of his.'

'How. . . ?'

There was no time to solve the puzzle. Slyke had somehow broken free, it seemed. Now there were more knocks at the door, more forceful. The old woman began to sob uncontrollably.

'Perhaps he freed Willie as well!' Carmalita said. 'There may be others we know nothing about. You must take Stony Harte away now!'

'Carmalita. . . .'

'No! I cannot go. I must take care of my sister and my poor mother. Go, Cameron Black, while there is time!'

Cameron locked his jaw and hastily searched the room as the pounding on the door grew more insistent. Emily moaned; Stony Harte began to stir. The gold was in Stony's saddle-bags, hidden beneath the bed. Cameron levered the heavy leather bags out from under the bed and tossed them out the window. It was moments only, but it seemed like uncountable hours before he was able to lift Stony Harte unceremoniously over the

133

sill and drop him to the ground below as well.

The banging at the front door continued and then there was the crack of splintering wood and Cameron knew that Slyke was in the house. He heard the scream of the old woman rise like a tortured fury and briefly he cursed himself for having brought pain into the old woman's last days. But it was not really he who had done it, but Stony Harte. If it hadn't been Cameron who had come, there would have been others one day – lawmen, treasure-seekers, old enemies from the outlaw trail.

Cameron managed to tie the saddle-bags on the jittery pinto pony's back and then to drape Harte, half-conscious and bound over the horse's withers before he swung into the saddle, and with pangs of regret, heeled the fresh, willing horse toward the desert flats beyond the hacienda.

The night was now cool, the wind unscented and dusty. The horse's leggy shadow stretched out before him as Cameron felt his way across the wasteland, having only a vague idea of where he was traveling. Once he heard a coyote howl and the answering yips of its pups, but something did not sound right about the animal calls, and he wondered if he was riding into Apache country unknowingly.

Harte's pony was a strong one and swift as outlaws need, but it began to slow noticeably as the moon grew higher over the sand dunes and Cameron swung down to give the animal a rest. Standing in the haunting landscape of wind-twisted dunes and scant broom, Cameron tried to take a bearing from the stars.

'Can't find your way, Poky?' Cameron heard Stony Harte murmur, and he looked to see Stony, still slung over the horse's neck, watching him with savage eyes. 'I thought it was you. Somehow. I don't know how you made it this far, but I knew it.' Stony's voice was gravelly but amused, if savage. 'You can't make your way across this desert without me, pal. I thought that I had taught you that. Without me you can't find your way out of a sand box. You're going to have to untie me. We can split what's left in those saddle-bags.'

Cameron didn't answer. He stood looking at the bleak, starrry, terrible night.

'You can't make it without me and you know it, Black.'

'Not the way you're traveling,' a strange, yet familiar voice interrupted. 'We at least need another horse.'

Cameron spun, his hand reaching for his pistol, but he was covered and knew there was no chance at all of shooting down the man who had emerged from the darkness.

'You!'

'Yes, it's me,' Elliot Hogan said, coming nearer. 'Voorman wasn't quite man enough to kill me. Hand me your gun.'

NINE

'I can't quite make up my mind what to do with either one of you,' Elliot Hogan was saying. The lanky, mustached man leaned back against the soft contour of the diamond-white dune and lit his cigar with the ember from their mesquite fire. Stony Harte said nothing, nor did Cameron Black.

'You see,' Hogan went on, with all the confidence a man who has the upper hand and knows it shows, 'I have the gold now – there's quite a pile missing by the way, Stony. You must pay your help well. But,' Hogan said, flicking the barrel of ash from the end of his cheroot, 'there's a reward for both of you men, dead or alive. You see, I have to weigh the benefits.

'First, I've had a long and fruitful relationship with Warden Traylor and Sheriff Yount. I've been paid well. But then,' he shrugged. And his face and eyes still showed the terrible marks of the Dutchman's beating, 'I'd have to share the gold if I took you in, wouldn't I?

'On the other hand,' Hogan said, as if he were lecturing them patiently, 'I could take you both back in dead rather than alive. But, God, boys! Do you know what a few days of desert heat can do to raise the stench? I'd have enough buzzards to blacken the sky following me.'

'Let me go,' Cameron said softly. 'You know by now that I had nothing to do with any of this.'

'Oh, son, you've everything to do with it. No matter what I decide you're at the heart of it, ready to pop up some day and give your version.'

'I wouldn't. . . .'

'I don't take any man at his word,' Hogan snapped. 'Of course you might decide to talk one day and so, you see, I have a problem here.'

'You've got the horses, I see,' Cameron said to change the subject. He watched the beaten-down army bay and the roan nuzzle futilely at the sand, looking for the smallest bit of vegetation. 'I wondered who took them.'

'That's right. I watered them down and gave them what graze I could while I waited for you to make a move. I walked out of those sandhills, Black. Walked! Through the heat storms of the day, the rocks cutting my boot leather to ribbons, my head exploding from the crazy Dutchman's bashing. You see, this is what I mean – I'm owed something. Fifty thousand in gold or, tilting it the other way, whatever small portion of it Yount and Warden Traylor feel like chipping off for me. I am the one who has done the work; they are the ones who get the gold. Yes, Black, that is what I mean when I say I do have a problem. I can become a wealthy outlaw like your friend here, or return to my menial occupation as a snitch. I don't care much for either option, to tell you the truth.'

'Kill us and get it over with,' Stony Harte grumbled. 'You talk too damn much for a lousy snitch. If you had the heart you'd be out there taking your money the way I do.'

Hogan looked challengingly into Stony Harte's eyes. Cameron had noticed the small movements Harte had been making throughout the conversation, but Hogan, concentrated on his own thoughts, had not.

'What makes you think you're so big?' Hogan asked, in a voice strangled with emotion.

'I *fight* for what I have; you just weasel for it,' Harte answered savagely.

Elliot Hogan upholstered his revolver and aimed it at Stony Harte's chest.

'You stinking Johnny Reb!' Hogan shouted, cocking his Colt.

As Hogan came to his feet, making his move,

Cameron recalled what he had seen earlier and it came into sharp focus. Stony Harte had been deliberately, carefully, working away on the knots binding his hands, probably planning an escape from Cameron himself. Now, as Hogan aimed the muzzle of his revolver at Harte, Stony sprang up and hurled himself at Hogan. The revolver exploded with fire in the night and Cameron saw Stony spin and cringe, holding his belly. But he did not stop his forward rush andd as he reached Elliot Hogan, the Colt fired again and the two went down against the sand in a heap. Again the gun muzzle shot flame, but this time its direction was downward and Hogan's body leaped and lay still.

Both men were motionless as Cameron approached them cautiously and kicked the gun away. He rolled Stony Harte on to his back and there was a sort of mad glee in Harte's eyes.

'You never thought I'd go out easily, did you, kid? He was meaning to kill both of us, you know?'

'I guess he. . . .' But there was no point in speaking more. Stony Harte was dead; Hogan was dead, and there was only the long empty night.

Cameron crawled away and fell face down against the sand. He didn't know what awakened him, but opening one eye he saw a high Apache moccasin not inches away, the pant legs of their typical white costume. He readied himself to die, but the Apaches, moving silently among them took neither scalps nor horses nor gold. Perhaps the scent of unhealthy death pushed them away from this angry scene.

In the morning, Cameron found himself alone. The dead had not gone, of course, but he did not touch them. The sand and the wind would complete their burial. He did pause long over Stony's body, wondering how he could retain a remote, strange sort of liking for this man who would have killed him.

Perhaps – perhaps there was some unknown connection between them, a blood tie no science could discern. Perhaps once, long ago, they had indeed shared an ancestor.

The roan and the bay horse Cameron set free to wander. Badly used and weak, their saddles were now stripped off and they were shooed away. Perhaps the Apaches would find them and have use for them. Perhaps they would wander awhile and find clear water and tall grass. Cameron hoped so; he had no further use for the suffering animals.

On the back of Stony Harte's strutting, strong, long-running pinto horse, the gold-laden saddle-bags across the animal's withers, he rode on, leaving the dead past behind, hoping for a better future.

TEN

There was no wind to speak of, only a light breeze that shifted the paint pony's mane and occasionally lifted loose sand from the peaks of the sculpted dunes. Cameron rode on, only half alert. The dead he had left behind but the future as he thought somberly on it, promised little more. He must place all of his trust in the Wells Fargo agent, Morton, and hope that the return of the stolen gold would be enough to allow him to keep his freedom. Matters would have been much simpler had he been able to bring Stony Harte in, but things had not worked according to plan.

The sand was blue-violet beneath the glow of the dwindling moon. The desert was not quite as barren now. Stands of greasewood and here and there tall ocotillo appeared as he guided the wearying paint horse toward Tucson and the Wells Fargo office there. His eyes felt gritty and the lids were heavy. He held the horse up one minute, repositioned the hat he had taken from beside Hogan and, patting the pony's neck, said, 'I know. We've got to have some rest. The morning heat will kill us if we don't stop soon.'

One of the horse's ears twisted back to listen to the meaningless words of this new rider. Cameron patted it again and they moved on another quarter of a mile only before they came upon a red-earth bluff protruding from the blanket of white sand. It was only nine or ten feet high, but it was in the right position to protect them from the glare of the morning sun. Cameron swung down heavily and laboriously unsaddled and slipped the paint's bit. The horse nuzzled the ground as if expecting forage or at least water, but there was none to be had.

Cameron folded the heavy horse blanket for a pillow and stretched out at the base of the red bluff, hoping the area was free of rattlesnakes. Then, not even caring about such things as his fatigue overwhelmed him, he tugged Hogan's hat over his face, folded his arms on his chest and went to sleep.

What woke him from his nearly comatose state he could not say, but Cameron blinked himself awake and stared into the emptiness. He thought he heard the slight shuffling sound of leather against sand. He sat up, drawing his gun. Yes – there it was! Something. A crooked shadow

143

against the backdrop of brilliant pre-dawn stars.

'Who's there?' he said in a low voice, and the shadowy figure came nearer. It was a man with a Winchester, that was clear now. He held it loosely, not aiming it at Cameron, but still he told him, 'Drop that rifle, stranger, I mean it.'

'It's empty,' came a rasping answer. 'Used all my rounds back there . . . got a few of them when they jumped me.' The man's words were slurred and he staggered as he came another step closer.

It was Slyke! 'I should've known it would be you,' the bald-headed man said. He sagged to the sand, placed the rifle aside and sat staring blankly at Cameron. 'I was hoping it was Stony. When I saw the horse. . . .'

He gasped painfully and removed his hand from his stomach so that Cameron could see the stub of an arrow protruding from his lower chest. 'Apaches jumped me.'

'I saw them,' Cameron answered. 'I was lucky they thought we were all already dead when they caught up.'

'Did the Indians get Stony?'

'No. A man named Hogan. He was following me hoping to find Stony and the gold.'

'I see,' Slyke said. He still had the marks of his fight with Cameron on his bald head. Now he lay back and stared upward into the night skies. Cameron moved to him, holstering his gun. Slyke was no longer a threat to anyone.

'You want me to try getting that arrow out of you, Slyke?'

'It's too late,' the gunman said, rolling his head from side to side. 'I'm awful thirsty, though.'

'I don't have any water, Slyke. I'm sorry.'

'I believe you are,' the bald man said. There was a silence between them for a long while. Cameron kept his eyes raised to the distances. If the Jicarillas had followed Slyke across the desert, there could be more trouble than he could handle coming at any minute.

A sudden thought occurred to Cameron. 'Slyke,' he said, shaking the bald man's shoulder. Slyke had closed his eyes as pain began to dominate him. Now he opened them halfway. His vision was clouded, but he seemed at least partly alert.

'Yeah?'

'Was Willie with you when you started after us?'

'No,' Slyke said, rolling his head. 'His mind was still fuzzy and he wasn't moving too well. You rang his bell pretty good.'

'He'll be coming along?'

'No, not old double-ugly,' Slyke said, with a laugh that broke into a blood-frothed cough. 'I told him I knew where you were going, that Stony and I could take back the gold easy from a greenhorn like you. Told him we'd meet him in

145

Mexico, little town we use all the time to hide out in between jobs. 'Course I was never going to Mexico if I got my hands on the gold. I was going to cross old scarface Willie. But he trusted my talk and him and fat Emily said they'd start for the border.'

'Emily!'

'Sure. One thing that sister of hers, that Carmalita, never understood: Emily likes this kind of life. The danger excites them, it seems. Some men seem born to follow the outlaw trail . . . and more than a few women.'

'What happened in the house, after I left?' Cameron wanted to know.

'All sorts of screaming and hair-pulling and the like. Emily's a lot bigger though and she fought that little Carmalita off and told her what she meant to do. The old woman . . . well, I'm sorry but she got so upset by the excitement that she had some kind of a stroke or heart attack. Last I seen 'em Emily was going to find Willie and the young one was sitting at her mother's bedside, crying with her head in her hands. You know, Cameron if . . .' Then there were no more 'ifs'. There would be no more 'ifs' for Slyke. He had died in the middle of the sentence and Cameron sat staring at the dead man, wondering just what it was that Slyke had meant to say and if it could have made any difference anyway.

Working in the darkness Cameron drew Slyke up against the side of the bluff and caved in some of it to make a crude cairn for the outlaw. Then, heavily, he saddled his horse and with dawn beginning to creep into the eastern skies, he started on toward Tucson to seek a finish to all of this.

Clarence Morton flung open the drapes that covered the windows of his upstairs office and with his thumbs hooked into the armholes of his vest, surveyed the morning scene as the residents of Tucson began to return to the day's life after the death of night. He ducked his head slightly to peer past the gilt lettering which spread across both windows in ornate script and read: 'Wells Fargo and Co.' Seeing the heavy lettering always gave him a feeling of substance and on this bright morning as he watched the early shoppers and lounging old-timers, the rolling hay wagons and businessmen in their high, stiff collars, he felt quite pleased with his position in the world. He rubbed idly at the widening bald circle on the crown of his head, frowned and then shrugged. It didn't matter – a man pays his price for his passage through life. A little less hair, a few wrinkles, an expanding belly. These are the unhappy residue of time expended pursuing success.

The sound of clomping boots in the outer

office was immediately followed by the exclamation of Morton's secretary – his wife's young nephew. He turned around sharply, glowering as the door was booted open and a roughly dressed young man with the dust of the desert on him entered his office without bothering to knock.

'See here!' Morton's secretary complained, but it was clear that the slender young man wanted little part of the sunburned, whiskered intruder.

'That's all right, David,' Morton said, as the visitor walked across the broad room, carrying a rifle in one hand, a heavy pair of saddle-bags slung over his shoulder.

'I've brought your gold back,' Cameron Black said, heaving the heavy leather bags onto Morton's desk where its impact sent several neatly stacked papers fluttering to the floor. The secretary in the doorway still watched, goggle-eyed, but Morton nodded at him again and he eased out of the room, drawing the door closed quietly.

'Hello, Mr Black. I didn't think I would ever be seeing you again.'

'Is your man off to call the law?' Cameron asked.

'David? No, sir, he does nothing unless I request it.' He paused, 'And then only half the time. Sit down, Mr Black.'

Cameron did. After leaning his rifle against the wall, he sprawled in a green leather chair across the desk from Morton who placed himself delicately in a sprung chair and folded his white hands together.

'The obvious question is why are you here?' the Wells Fargo agent said.

'For that.' Cameron nodded at the gold-filled saddle-bags. 'That isn't mine and I don't want to be hunted for it. You, I have reluctantly decided, are the only man of standing with anything approaching ethical straightness.'

'I see,' Morton answered. 'You mean that there are others among the "powers-that-be" you do not find trustworthy?'

'What do you think?' Cameron said harshly. 'Look, you might not be at the sorry level Warden Traylor, Hogan or Sheriff Yount are at. You seem to have some sort of moral courage. I think your willingness to go along with such a bunch of greedy bastards is that you are sincere in your attempt to protect your employer's assets.'

'That's what you think, is it?' Morton asked carefully. The morning sun grew warm on the back of his balding skull.

'That's what I think, yes.'

'Well, Mr Black,' Morton said with a sigh, as he leaned forward to place folded hands on his desk, one finger toying with a buckle on the saddle-bags, 'you are right in your conjecture.' He held up a hand as Cameron started to blurt out a hasty answer. 'In your shoes I would be harsh in my judgement of me as well.

'But, Mr. Black. I am in a position of watching over all shipments which our company *guarantees*. This is a lawless and a dangerous land as you know. At times,' he said, rubbing the bridge of his nose, 'I have taken extreme measures to try protecting the company, which, after all, is my job. I have used informers and even strong-arm tactics. I am proud of none of this, but were you in *my* shoes you would understand why it has been done. . . . I see you don't like my explanation.

'Yuma Prison is run by thugs and brigands, Mr Black, as you have discovered. I have no choice but work with the rougher elements.'

Cameron held up a weary hand and said to the Wells Fargo man, 'Listen, Morton, I don't care to know how you salve your conscience. I should be feeling hostile toward you, but I'm not. Anymore. I am too tired of all of this to even care. All I want from you is two things.'

'Yes?' Morton said, now eager to please. 'A reward, of course.'

'No reward,' Cameron said, squinting into the bright sunlight which angled through the office windows and formed shadows of their lettering against the walls and floor. 'I want, first of all, a receipt for the gold. And I want something on the

Wells Fargo stationery completely exonerating me and thanking me for my co-operation.'

'That's all?' Morton asked with some surprise.

'That's all. I just want to continue with my life.'

'I see . . . yes. How much of the shipment is here, Mr Black?'

'I have no idea. I haven't even glanced at it. I suggest you have your secretary or someone else count it and put it in that letter I requested.'

'It started out as a fifty-thousand dollar shipment,' Morton said doubtfully, returning to his old practices.

'Yes, I understand that,' Cameron told him, leaning forward now to place his own forearms on Morton's desk, his hat thumbed far back. 'This is my understanding of what happened – the scrip was virtually worthless off an army post and so Stony Harte burned the lot. The silver is still in a strongbox somewhere along your line. If your witness can show you where the robbery occurred a dozen men with shovels might eventually find it. Stony buried it because he was riding alone and by the pound it wasn't worth enough to make it worth his trouble. Any missing gold was handed around to the rest of his gang to buy drink and women with.'

'I see.' Morton looked down and then seemed to brighten a little. 'The scrip, of course is unimportant. The army can print that tissue up in any amount they like, so long as we assure them that this batch has been irretrievably lost. The silver . . . as you say, there is still a chance that it can be recovered.

'How much gold did you say was missing, Mr Black?'

'I told you I never looked at it, let alone counted it.'

'Then you'll want to be here when the banker, my secretary and I count it.'

'Why in hell would I even care?' Cameron Black asked coldly. 'Just see that those letters are drafted before I leave this room.'

'Yes, of course,' Morton said, now seeming greatly relieved. 'Still Wells Fargo would like you to have some small reward.'

'I never want to touch that money. I've seen what it can do.' Pondering silently for a minute as his head drooped slowly with exhaustion he finally murmured, 'There is one thing I would like – if you can see to it.'

'Anything.'

'At Yuma Prison. In the stables there is a gray mare with a white mane and tail. Her owner's deceased. I'd kind of like her for my own if you could tether her behind one of your stages and lead her up that spur line to Tombstone.'

Morton smiled with relief. He had had no idea what Cameron was going to ask for. He made himself a note on a fresh sheet of paper. 'That we can do for you, Mr Black. Tombstone? That's where you're going, is it? Have you ever been there before?'

'No, sir,' Cameron Black answered. 'That's why I'm going.'

Cameron was virtually walking in his sleep as Morton summoned his nephew to go find the local banker so that they could tally up the gold, and he just managed to get the pinto horse stabled up and to check in at the hotel where he fell asleep without undressing, happy in the knowledge that he would at least have Dolly with him if he were ever forced to ride that lonesome desert west of Tombstone again.

ELEVEN

'Not today Mr Black, sorry.'

The pale Arizona skies were streaked with only the faintest of cloud haze drifting over Tombstone on a quiet and bright morning. Cameron Black had not yet eaten, but he was eagerly awaiting Dolly's arrival and his nights had not been calm since the trials of the desert. He awoke at midnight and stared out at the beautifully primitive landscape beyond the rough town and could not fall back to sleep.

'I told you,' the Wells Fargo agent said, his elbows resting on the scarred station counter. 'That Yuma spur, they don't run it but every other day. So by the time they change at Tucson to switch teams, another day's lost. Soonest your horse can be in is tomorrow morning. I already told your wife there the same thing twice.'

'My . . .' Cameron blinked and turned uncertainly. In the corner of the office where dust motes danced in the morning sunlight stood Carmalita.

She took a hesitant step forward. The office manager asked, 'Did I speak out of turn?' but neither answered him.

Cameron felt as if his boots had been nailed to the floor. He lifted a hand and then took one step. Carmalita threw herself into his arms impetuously and then stepped back, turning her face away with embarrassment.

'I can't . . .' she began.

'Let's step outside,' Cameron said, holding her hand as they walked to the door, the station agent musing.

Outside it was relatively cool, no more than eighty degrees in the shade of the buildings. They walked a little way down the avenue on the board-walk, waited for a freight wagon to pass and then went to the small dusty park in the center of town where they seated themselves, Carmalita uncertainly smoothing the skirt of the black dress she wore. Mourning clothes.

'Your mother?' Cameron asked.

'Yes,' Carmalita said.

'I'm sorry.'

'You did not cause it,' Carmalita said.

'No? Maybe I had a hand in it, though.'

'It was evil men and their gold,' Carmalita said, and he did not answer, because she was right.

'My sister has gone away,' she said sadly. 'I will not see her ever again.'

'You tried to prevent it,' he replied, taking her hand.

'Yes, but maybe I was wrong to interfere in her affairs; maybe it is always a mistake to try to guide people in a different direction from the one they have chosen.'

Again Cameron didn't answer. Maybe Carmalita was right at that, but her heart had been in the right place.

'Mother did not live to see the morning,' Carmalita said speaking to the ground. A mockingbird with white-banded wings and cocky expression landed nearly at her feet, looking up as if expecting a treat and then angrily sped away. 'We buried her in the little cemetery in the pueblo. I realized I had no place to go. No! I lie, Cameron – I knew there was one place I wanted to go above all others. I knew that you wanted to come to Tombstone if you could survive the desert once more.

'And so,' she said in a small voice. 'I came here first.'

'I'm glad. . . .' Words failed him. 'How did you know about Dolly?'

'Who? Oh, the horse. I knew if you were successful in your battle that Wells Fargo would have to be involved in some way and so I became friendly with the little man you met in the office. He told me that, yes, he knew your name because the district supervisor had telegraphed him to make certain that your horse was delivered to you here without delay.'

'Morton.'

'I do not know. But that made my heart beat faster because I knew you had reached Tucson. I knew you were coming here. Why else would your horse Dolly be coming? Each morning I asked the man about your horse and the man in the office explained matters to me. I—' She turned her face down again, 'I lied and I told him that I was your wife, Cameron, so he would not think I was a crazy woman!'

'I see,' he said, and then he leaned her head against his shoulder with a strong, gentle hand.

'Cameron?' she asked, looking up with those liquid brown eyes. 'Have you had luck here?'

He laughed. 'It depends on what you call luck! I am going to work as a muleteer next Tuesday.'

'That does not pay much money, does it, Cameron?'

'Not a whole lot. I'll work my way up into something.'

'I know you will. Cameron?' She pushed away from him enough to search his eyes thoroughly. 'A mule-skinner man, whatever you call them . . . he must be away from home often.'

'Now and then.'

'I thought so,' Carmalita said. 'And the work –
is it dangerous?'

'Sometimes, they tell me.'

'I thought all of this was so,' she said. 'Then I
would be in your way, Cameron, is that not true?
A crazy woman standing behind you somewhere
on the trail, wanting you to come home?'

He laughed again, freely, and held her tight.
'My Carmalita – that's all any man works to have!'